Longing and Belonging
By
SJ Ronayne

DCL Publications, LLC
www.dclpublications.biz

Peter

First Edition February 2010

DCL Publications
1033 Plymouth Dr.
Grafton, OH 44044

ISBN 978-0-9844615-3-0

PUBLISHED IN THE UNITED STATES OF AMERICA

To my parents, who have always supported my love of books - even when I was too young for the books I was reading and writing!

Table of Contents

Bedeviling Dulcie

Chapter One

Lady Dulcie Brighton sat in the corner of the ballroom, her mother her only company. She tried to sigh but couldn't take a deep enough breath. The stays of her corset dug into her hips, chest, and under her arms. Her only thought was that of getting home and taking off the damn thing. Viscount Stanby passed, deigning her with a polite but distant nod.

"Mother, can we not leave? Please?"

Her mother, still lovely and vibrant at the age of three and fifty, tsked. "You haven't been on the dance floor once this evening."

"Well, I would, Mother, but it would be a bit strange, dancing by myself." Dulcie huffed in exasperation. She loved her mother dearly and on any other occasion would be happy to sit and be her company, but she could no longer do it tonight. "Mother, my dance card is empty. Let me walk out of here with a tiny shred of dignity."

As Dulcie saw it, if she left early, no one would know for certain her card didn't have even a single name on it. It would appear she was feeling sour and decided to leave before any possible suitors were able to make their way to her.

"Dulcie!" She cringed as her friend, Caressa, called out to her.

Lady Caressa Davenport, only daughter and youngest child to the Duke of Courtney, was flitting her way to Dulcie's corner. Dulcie's father, the Duke of Rothshire, had been friends with Caressa's father at University. If it hadn't been for lifelong exposure, Dulcie wondered, would the slim, effervescent Caressa be the friend of plump, dowdy Dulcie?

With her ethereal blond hair, Wedgwood blue eyes, and fairy-like body, Caressa was everything a woman should be. With Dulcie's heavy copper strands, mud brown eyes, and body to rival that of the walrus housed at the menagerie, she was far from what the men of the ton were looking for in a wife. The idea of what one would think of the body she had to look upon in the mirror everyday made her sigh again.

Caressa claimed the seat to her right and grabbed Dulcie's hand. "Isn't this wonderful?"

"Hmm," Dulcie replied noncommittally. For the first time she noticed the two men Caressa had in tow. One was Malcolm Tripford, the Viscount of Trewston. Handsome, tall, with dark blond hair and piercing gray eyes, and a considerable fortune, he was considered one of the top catches of the Season. Next to him was the Honorable Kirkland Perry, the oldest son of the Baron of Xander. He had curly brown hair, green eyes, and stood to inherit a not so small estate himself. He had a kind smile, which was more than could be said for Malcolm, who only seemed to tolerate her presence because she was a friend of Caressa's and the daughter of a Duke. And, though he was not as handsome as Malcolm, Kirkland was still an attractive man.

A new song started and the Viscount cleared his throat. "I do believe this dance is mine, Lady Davenport."

Caressa giggled into Dulcie's hand and leaned over to tell her that the Viscount had claimed more than half of the evening's dances. Dulcie smiled and patted her friend's hand. "Then you had best not disappoint him."

She extricated her hand from Caressa's and made shooing motions. Caressa giggled again and spirited off with the man. Kirkland watched them drift off and Dulcie wondered if the man had claimed the other half of Caressa's card. As if remembering she was there, Kirkland turned and smiled down at her.

"Are you enjoying the party, Duchess? Lady Brighton?"

Her mother nodded serenely, as if relieved a man was finally speaking to Dulcie. Dulcie nodded as well. "Lord and Lady Wrenley certainly outdid the Earl of Stockton's soiree."

Kirkland laughed gently. "Indeed, and the Earl is simply steaming about it." He looked around until he located the man of whom they spoke, and pointed him out to Dulcie. "Never mind that his daughter is one of the most coveted girls of the Season. The Baron had the gall to out perform a superior."

When he looked back at Dulcie, Kirkland was silent for a moment. She watched as a blush crept up his neck, over his jaw and into his cheeks. "I am, of course, speaking to the most coveted," he murmured.

Dulcie blushed in embarrassment. It was obvious Kirkland was trying to be nice, but did he have to make her feel even more inadequate? "It's all right, Mr. Perry."

An uncomfortable silence stretched between them and Kirkland looked around. The wispy Miss Leticia Downey floated past and snagged Kirkland's attention. He looked after her before looking back to Dulcie. She smiled, her heart tugging a bit as she nodded, relieving him of standing guard. He bowed over Dulcie's hand and took off in the direction of the magistrate's daughter.

Dulcie uncrossed and re-crossed her ankles, silently cursing the slippers, which fell off her feet yet again. She sat through another two dances, seeing more of her friends twirl by in the arms of handsome, wealthy, and enamored gentlemen. Whenever one spotted her, she'd smile as though nothing were wrong, even waving occasionally.

It wasn't unknown to her friends that she had yet to have even one gentleman caller, let alone an offer for her hand. Nor had it escaped anyone's notice that the end of the Season was drawing near. It was looking as though she'd be back next year, with another line of younger girls and unappreciative men. As it was, this was her fourth time out and if she didn't receive any attention this time, she feared her parents would insist on making a match for her. Dulcie shuddered to think to whom they would sell her.

She was about to suggest to her mother, again, that they leave, when someone behind her said, "There's our girl! See, I told you we would find her."

It was her brother, William's voice. She turned to find her two older brothers, one older sister, and their spouses. Miles, third in birth order stepped away from his very pregnant wife, Arian, and kissed the top of her head. Elaine, second oldest, hugged her tightly, before William kissed her cheek.

"So, Pixie, how has the evening been?"

Dulcie was about to answer but was cut off by a hastily covered snicker. The second son of the Duke of Stromworth cleared his throat before glancing at them and walking quickly away. Dulcie could feel her cheeks heating. She had heard many such snickers over her family's pet name for her. Ever oblivious, her brothers and sisters awaited her answer. She pasted as wide a smile as she could muster across her face. "Wonderful."

"Good. Would you like anything to drink, Pixie?"

"They have some lovely punch on the table on the other side of the room."

Her brother-in-law, Daniel, patted her hand before kissing her sister's knuckles. "Would you like some, love?"

"That would be lovely. I'll wait with Mother and Pixie."

Miles helped Arian onto a chair and kissed the tip of his wife's nose. Elaine settled next to her and William's wife, Reagan, sat on the opposite side of Dulcie, between her and her mother. The three men left and her sisters began chattering immediately.

"They're going in the wrong direction," Dulcie announced.

Regan looked after them. "Are they?"

"They'll find their way to the punch, Dulcie. Anyway, the longer they have to look, the longer we get to talk, just us girls." Arian smiled, smoothing her hands over her distended belly.

Elaine grabbed up both of Dulcie's hands. "So? Who have you bewitched this season?"

Dulcie smiled, another tug pulling at her heart. "Oh, you know Pixie, Elaine. She probably has a dozen suitors vying for her attention," Arian said in her dulcet voice.

Dulcie knew her sisters weren't trying to be cruel, but their encouragement merely served to reminder her, that at the ripe age of twenty-three, Dulcie was beginning to approach the shelf. She looked around in time to see Stromworth walking quickly past them, tugging his jacket and smoothing his hair. Moments later, her brothers returned with glasses for the five women.

When Daniel bent near, Dulcie whispered, "What did you three do?" Her brother-in-law had the nerve to smile and wink before straightening to stand behind her sister's chair. She groaned into her punch glass.

Her siblings and their spouses chattered at her. Dulcie nodded, made the occasional sound that could be interpreted as either a sound of agreement or dissention.

"Damn it all."

"Miles!" Their mother admonished her brother for his curse.

"Sorry," he murmured. He, William, and Daniel were all looking to the front of the room. Dulcie stood to see what could have caused her brother to damn anything.

Suddenly, the room was too small. Nausea began to rise from the pit of her belly. "I need some air," Dulcie whispered. She broke away from her family and headed for the French doors behind them.

She burst through and walked down the length of the balcony. At the end, she took a deep breath, easier standing up than sitting, before falling onto a small stone bench. Tall topiaries stood to either side, and blessedly blocked her view of the ballroom. Miles had been right. Damn it all.

*   *   *

Jackson Cornell, Marquess of Torningate, watched the silken copper hair flee the room. He swung his gaze back to the doors of the ballroom. Bartel. Of course.

He walked out onto the balcony. Perhaps now was time to approach the duke's lovely daughter. He could make her out on the bench. Light dappled her face and chest as it filtered through the plants between her and the windows. He pulled a cheroot and match from his breast pocket, clamped the thin cigar between his lips and struck the match.

"Oh!"

Her husky voice floated to him, seeping into his pores before tightening his skin all over his body.

"My goodness, my Lord, you scared me half to death."

"My Lord?" he taunted her. Since taking on the responsibilities of his father's lesser title, Dulcie had been much more formal with him. It saddened him that a woman once so genuine and open toward him now distanced herself. Especially when it was the last thing he wanted.

"What would you have me call you, then?" Her peevish return made him want to laugh.

"Oh, I don't know. Jackson? Jack? Even Cornell would be preferable. One you called me in social settings. Another when only our families were together. The last, when you were so annoyed you couldn't even think straight enough to call me one of the first two."

He smiled as he stepped up to her. So as not to spook her, he leaned a hip against the stone balustrade rather than sit next to her on the bench.

Her perfect front stayed up for another second before that beautiful, soft smile of hers touched her full pink lips. "Of course. How are you, Jackson?"

"I was doing quite well until someone allowed a boar into the room."

"What?"

"Hmm, yes, this one runs around in the guise of a peer. Blond hair, black eyes. Looks up as many skirts as he can?"

Understanding settled over Dulcie's beautiful features. "Well, if he has papers, one can't very well refuse him, can one," she murmured.

"Like hell."

"Jackson, please. There's really no point."

He tried not to let his irritation at her tired tone show on his face. He pulled in a puff of aromatic smoke and released it. "You shouldn't feel you must leave a room simply because some fool has arrived, Dulcie."

"Perhaps if said fool had proposed to you as part of some colossal joke, you'd want to flee his presence as well. Cornell."

He loved how she added his last name as an afterthought, letting him know he had annoyed her. Jack dropped his cigar and held out his opposite hand to her. "Come on, Dulcie. Let's show him he's nothing more than a speck. After all, he may be a Baron but you were born of a Duke and Duchess," Jackson said with a smile.

Dulcie chewed her bottom lip and Jack was hard-pressed not to do it for her. She reached out hesitantly. Crushing the glowing, forgotten stick under his boot heel, Jack pulled her to her feet and they walked back into the room just as a waltz began. "Why, I do believe this dance is mine, Lady Dulcie."

She smiled and shook her head but allowed him to lead her out to the dance floor. She moved beautifully with him. "See, now you're the center of attention. Just as it should be."

Glorious cinnamon eyes peered out from under thick black lashes and her cheeks and ears pinkened delightfully. He loved when her porcelain skin blushed. It covered not just her cheeks and perfectly shaped ears, but also crept down her chest and Jack wondered where else her skin heated.

When the dance ended, Jack reluctantly returned Dulcie to her family. She carefully extracted her hand from his arm. "There, Mother, I've danced. May we leave now?"

"Oh, all right, Dulcie." Her mother rose from the chair with much grace.

"I'll walk you fair ladies out."

"Oh, Jackson, no. It's all right."

"I insist, Dulcie."

She ducked her head but didn't argue further. After helping them into their carriage, Jackson no longer felt like staying, either. He was on his way to his transport when someone called his name.

"Jack?"

He turned to find Dulcie's brothers walking toward him. "Will, Miles, Daniel. How may I help you?"

William spoke up first. "We were wondering at that performance you were putting on in the ballroom."

The Great Wall, these three were. "I thought my lifelong friend deserved to have at least one dance. Especially when the peacock was present."

William looked to his brothers and they nodded. "All right. Good night, Jack."

"Good night, gentlemen." His coachman opened his door and lowered the step for Jack to climb in. As they drove away, Jack laughed at the antics of Dulcie's brothers.

Chapter Two

"Hello?"

"It's us, darling. How are you feeling tonight?" Moira Brighton bent and kissed her husband's cheek. She pulled back abruptly as he sneezed into his handkerchief. "Have you eaten anything tonight?"

"That evil minion of yours forced his broth down my throat earlier," Abraham croaked.

Moira laughed softly as she stroked her husband's shoulders. He sighed as she pressed into the stiff muscles. Dulcie entered the room, kissed each of their cheeks and bid them good night.

"Well, wait a moment, now. How did the evening go?"

Their youngest child pressed her hand to her forehead. "Please, father, let us save this for tomorrow. My head aches miserably."

The duke sighed and nodded. "Good night, dearling," Abe said through a stuffed up nose.

"Good night, Papa."

Moira listened until she heard her daughter's door close. She circled the armchair in which her husband sat and settled on the footstool in front of him. "Oh, darling, I have wonderful news."

"What, my love?"

"I believe I know who we can get to marry Dulcie."

"Oh?"

Moira nodded excitedly. "Jack!"

"Who?"

She huffed. "Jackson Cornell."

"Little Jack? You can't be serious. He's little more than a child."

Moira squinted at her husband, looking into his eyes. "Give it to me."

Abe looked around unconvincingly. "What?"

"The flask, darling. You shouldn't drink when you're ill."

"Oh, humbug." Abe grumbled but handed his silver flask to his wife. She pulled a key from the small bag looped over her wrist, unlocked the cabinet in the corner, and deposited her husband's contraband into it before relocking the doors.

"Jackson is a fully grown man now, love. You forget he's nearly Elaine's age."

He seemed to be in thought for a moment. "I suppose he must be. But why do you think we should give him our little pixie?"

Moira began to pace before her husband. "Because, Abe, she isn't a pixie anymore. She is three and twenty. This is her fourth season when, in all rights, it should be her sixth or seventh. Jackson hasn't offered for anyone's hand and at nearly thirty, he must begin thinking about an heir.

"Dulcie will be at William's tomorrow. While she's there, we'll ask for Jack to come here and we'll put it to him."

"Dulcie will be angry if she finds out we did this."

"Then we'll have to make sure she doesn't find out until after the wedding." She knelt next to his chair and took hold of his hand. "Please, Abraham. It pains me to watch all those little...little...bastards hurt our baby girl by ignoring her in favor of girls nowhere near her."

He smiled down at her, that indulgent smile she loved so well. "All right darling. Pen him a note tonight. If we get it to him now, he may just agree to come over tomorrow afternoon."

Moira squealed and hugged her husband. She dashed off to write the note, but turned back at the last minute. "The moment you're all better, love, you had best be ready." She sent him a lascivious smile.

Abe laughed in response. "Go. And send your minion to help me get upstairs."

"Oliver! Take the duke to his room and return to me in his office." Moira called out as she practically ran to her husband's office.

"Yes, my Lady."

She wrote her missive and handed it to Oliver once he returned downstairs.

"I'll have it sent over right away, madam."

"Thank you, Oliver."

Oliver bowed and left the office. Moira sat in one of the wing chairs in front of the fireplace, writing pad and pencil in hand. She had much planning to do.

* * *

Jack knocked on the front door of the London townhouse he had spent many a day at in his childhood. He looked at the note Lady Moira had sent to his own home the night before. *A matter of terrible importance.* He had no idea what could be so serious, but if Dulcie's family needed something of him, he was only too ready to provide a solution.

When the missive arrived at his home so early this morning, Jack had been stunned. The urgent knocking had had his tired mind dreaming it was Dulcie, there to beg him to take her into his arms and his bed. When he saw the note in the decidedly not-Dulcie footman's hand, his hopes had risen that at least the note was from Dulcie. Instead, it had been from her mother. So, in his perhaps misguided devotion to their lovely youngest child, here Jack stood. The door swung open, admitting him.

The butler took his calling card and Jack waited in the foyer while the man delivered it. Oliver returned in less than a minute. "This way, your Lordship."

Lady Moira greeted him with a kiss on the cheek. Jack gently shook the duke's hand. "Come now, boy. I'm ill, not dying."

Jack smiled and gripped the older man's hand harder than before. He sat in the chair the butler indicated and Oliver asked if they would like some tea. "That would be lovely, Oliver. Thank you." Lady Moira replied.

When the man left the room and shut the doors behind him, Jack looked to the couple. "What can I do for you?"

Lady Moira looked to her husband and back to Jack. "Tell us, Jackson. You're fond of our daughter, yes?"

Intriguing. "Dulcie?" Jack asked for clarification. The lady looked to her husband, a note of uncertainty on her face this time, before returning her gaze to Jack. She nodded. Jack smiled gently. "Yes, my Lady, I am fond of her."

Lady Moira and Lord Abraham both beamed at him. Oliver returned with a tea cart. Once he poured and provided each of them with a biscuit, he was gone again. The duke's wife was shaking as she placed her cup on the side table. When she looked back to Jack, the uncertainty from before had returned.

"Understand, Jack. We love our daughter very much, and we would do anything to make her happy."

"Dulcie deserves happiness."

Her parents nodded and the duke spoke. "Tell us, Jack. Have you met any young ladies this season for whom you think you might set your cap?"

Jack shook his head. Lord Abraham continued. "And don't you think perhaps it is time you married and started a family?"

Shock rolled through him. Here Jack had thought he'd ask for their daughter's hand and they were giving it away! "Of course, I do."

Lady Moira took control again. "We were thinking, Jackson. You and Dulcie get on so well. You need an heir, and Dulcie, though she has never said it, wants so badly to be a mother. What would you say if we suggested you marry our daughter?"

Jack had never felt such a sensation in his life. His stomach clenched, his palms dampened, and he had to readjust himself to hide the evidence of his agreeability to their idea. "I care a great deal for Dulcie, and, in all honesty, can't imagine a better woman to bear the next Marquess of Torningate."

"Oh, Jackson, that is wonderful!" Lady Moira rose and wrapped her arms around his shoulders.

Jack smiled and patted her forearm before she released him. When she was again seated beside her husband, Jack clapped and rubbed his hands together. "So, should we prepare a contract now, or wait until Dulcie joins us?"

Lord Abraham spoke again. "There's another thing we would ask of you."

If it was as good as their first request, Jack knew he'd not refuse them. "Yes?"

"We do not want Dulcie to know we have gone around her to make this match, so we ask that you make it appear that you want this match. We would like you to woo our daughter." Abraham looked a tad uncomfortable with his request but made it anyway.

Jack sat back for a moment. Dulcie didn't know her parents were asking him to marry her. If she didn't know, she hadn't asked them to set this meeting. What if she didn't want what they were asking? What if she didn't want him?

Well, he'd just have to convince her she did want him. "There will not be a person in England who doesn't know I am out to marry Dulcie."

Her parents smiled, seemingly relieved. After drinking his tea, Jack bid Dulcie's parents goodbye. They made plans to meet at Lord Higgins's ball that evening. When Dulcie looked at her card tonight, she would find every dance filled. With his name on each line.

Normally, Jack disdained high fashion, preferring comfort, but for the ball, he acquired a new suit, new Hessian boots, and trimmed his thick black hair. His final purchases were made at a flower cart. There he bought a rose for his lapel and several blossoms of freesia. He held the delicate white flowers to his nose and breathed deep of the scent that always brought the image of Dulcie to mind. All year round, she smelled of the heady flower. And one day, that scent would cover his bed and sated body as well.

At the ball that evening, Jack waited impatiently for Dulcie's arrival. Finally, her and her mother's names were announced. He slipped his hand into his pocket. Fingering the dance card he had already filled with his name, he approached the two.

"Good evening, ladies."

"Good evening, Jackson," Lady Moira replied.

Dulcie was distracted. Looking over her place setting, she frowned. "Mmm, yes, good evening, Jackson."

"Is something wrong?" He asked.

Dulcie smiled as she looked at him. "No. I suppose they have merely decided not to waste a dance card on me."

Jack didn't know which bothered him more – that Dulcie believed their hosts would do such a thing or that the thought didn't seem to affect her much at all. He reached into his pocket and pulled out the beribboned paper.

"Hold out your hand." She did and he tied the emerald silk around her wrist.

She looked surprised. As she was about to open it, Jack took Dulcie's hand and led her onto the dance floor. He pulled her into his arms as the next song began. "I do believe this is my dance."

Jack only allowed her to sit once dinner was served. He sat at her table and told stories of his time spent traveling before he was called home when his father had fallen ill. He told her of Africa and the Orient.

When the dancing resumed, Jack took her hand to lead her back to the dance floor. He led her around and around until she begged for mercy. He agreed and led Dulcie into an alcove created by one of the ballroom's cathedral windows and heavy brocade curtains. Jack leaned against the window and Dulcie took a seat on a padded velvet upholstered bench.

She was so beautiful. Her violet dress looked black in the dim light of their enclosure. Moonlight sparkled off the garment's beadwork and made her skin glow. Dulcie looked up at him and he smiled, feeling oddly shy at having been caught ogling her.

"You know, Jackson, if you dance with only me tonight, people will think you're courting me."

"Only think it, Dulcie? That simply won't do."

She frowned. "What?"

Jack got on his knee beside her. "After tonight, not a single person in that room, nor the whole of England, will question my intentions toward you."

Even in the moonlight, Jack could see Dulcie's cheeks color. She sputtered indignantly. "What are you talking about, Cornell? You have no intentions toward me."

"On the contrary, lovely Dulcie, I intend to make you mine."

"Ha! Since when?" Her ire was rising and Jack loved it.

"For a long time now, Dulcie. For a very long time." Before she could say anymore, Jack leaned forward and captured her mouth with his.

*   *   *

Oh, my goodness. Dulcie couldn't believe what was happening. Jackson Cornell had his mouth pressed softly against hers so that his lips surrounded her top lip as hers surrounded his bottom one. His fingertips came up and brushed her cheek. She had never felt anything so sweet as Jack's kiss. He pulled away and Dulcie whimpered, but he was merely repositioning his head.

When he returned, the kiss invoked a hunger she had never known she possessed. Jack pressed his tongue forward and licked her bottom lip before pushing against her teeth. Dulcie moaned and opened her mouth. Jackson hummed his approval and found her tongue with his. As he rubbed the wonderfully textured surface against every bit of her mouth, his hand left her cheek to stroke down her neck. When he reached the base, his hand covered much of her bare upper chest.

Jack pulled away again, this time kissing his way to her ear. "I'm going to touch you, Dulcie. I have to. I've waited so long to have you in my arms, I have to touch you."

"Where?" Dulcie asked breathlessly.

"Your breast, Dulcie." His deep voice was thicker than usual and it sounded as though she was not the only one having trouble breathing. "I'm only going to hold you in my hand, but if we had somewhere more private, I would kiss it. I would lick your skin and suck on your nipple, Dulcie."

As he spoke his hand covered her breast, warming her through the layers of her dress and her shift and the new corset her dress maker had convinced her was the height of fashion. Jack continued speaking and Dulcie thought she just might swoon. "I would nibble on it, bite down hard then lick the pain away." He squeezed and Dulcie's breath stuck in her throat.

Jack turned his face into her throat and licked her skin before asking, "What color are your nipples, Dulcie?"

"What?" She couldn't make her brain work. It sounded like he was speaking underwater.

"Your nipples, Dulcie. What color are they?"

She swallowed hard. Jackson knowing the color of her nipples seemed exceedingly more intimate than his touches, but she wanted to tell him. She needed to. "They are dark pink," she whispered. "Almost red. And they hurt so much right now, Jackson. They are tight and hard."

Jackson growled and squeezed harder, this time catching her nipple between his thumb and forefinger. Dulcie would have screamed at the exquisite pleasure it sent from her breast to her womb had Jackson not chosen that precise moment to kiss her again. This kiss was more demanding than the ones before. He pressed her mouth open as wide as it would go and plunged his tongue in and out of her mouth. Then she realized his hips were moving against her thigh in exactly the same rhythm; that the juncture of her thighs throbbed right along with his movements. She felt an unusual trickling sensation.

Dulcie reached up. One hand covered his at her breast, pressing him closer, positioning his fingers where they could pinch her again. Her other hand landed on the soft fabric of his shirt. She touched his chest, pressing her fingers into the firm flesh before smoothing up to his neck and tangling in his hair.

He caught her nipple again, this time squeezing and releasing in time to his thrusting tongue and hips. She whimpered again and began moving her hips, trying to rub the strangely pinched spot between her legs. She pulled his hand from her breast and began to guide it down her stomach. Dulcie desperately needed Jack to stop the throbbing below but he pulled his hand away and sat back from her.

Dulcie tried to pull him back into her arms but he shook his head. Jack stood and turned to the window, pressing his body against the glass. She stood, finding it very hard to get her legs to hold her. When they finally held steady she walked up and stood next to him, pressing her cheek to the cold pane. He opened his beautiful hazel eyes and Dulcie found herself unable to keep the contact. "I'm sorry, Jackson."

He laughed. "You have nothing to apologize for, Dulcie."

Dulcie moved away from the window, crossing the tight space to peek through the curtains. She dropped the fabric and asked, "Then, why did you stop?"

Jackson came up behind her. His hands settled on her shoulders and his chin came to rest in the curve where her neck met her shoulder. "Because, if I didn't stop, I was going to make love to you right here, with all of London on the other side of that fabric, and I wouldn't have cared a single bit." He kissed her neck and Dulcie shivered. "You mean too much to me, Dulcie. So, while I have the presence of mind to let you go, walk out. I'll follow when I've gotten a hold of myself."

Unable to stop herself, she turned into his arms and rose onto her toes. Not nearly as experienced or knowledgeable as Jackson, Dulcie just pressed her lips to his. His hands came up and cupped her face. He didn't advance the contact anymore than that, just touched her skin, and only barely. Dulcie slowly stepped away from him, not taking her eyes from Jackson's until she had to step out of the alcove and onto the dance floor.

Dulcie returned to her mother's side. She knew her cheeks should be flaming and shame should be filling her, but Dulcie couldn't summon one single bad feeling from what had happened. Jackson had kissed her, and touched her. He wanted to marry her.

A smile pulled at her lips and she wondered when they could next be alone.

*   *   *

Jack handed Lady Moira up into their carriage. With her mother inside, Jack turned to Dulcie. She was looking at him shyly through her lashes. Unable to resist touching her, he took her hand in his and kissed her knuckles, keeping his lips on her hand longer than etiquette deemed proper. Dulcie tilted her chin up and smiled at him, soft and intimate; it felt like a kick to his chest and a stroke to his cock. He handed Dulcie up and closed the door.

Lady Moira looked out. "Jackson, the duke and I would love to have you over for the evening on Wednesday."

"Would anyone else like my company for the evening?"

Dulcie moved aside the window curtain, leaving her face silhouetted in the moonlight. "I would enjoy it greatly if you would come."

Though he understood Dulcie didn't know what she said could be taken out of context, Jack hardened knowing he would enjoy it greatly, too. "Then I shall be there."

"Six o'clock, then?" Lady Moira asked.

"Six," Jackson agreed. He stepped back and the carriage rolled out of the drive.

Jack turned to find Dulcie's brothers waiting for him. "You and Dulcie were missing for some time, Cornell," Will said darkly.

"Care to tell us what you're up to?" Miles asked.

"Not at all, *brothers*. Not at all."

The three men looked to one another. Jack started to make his way to his own carriage. Daniel spoke as the men followed him. "It might be bad form to beat him. At the moment, anyhow."

The other two murmured their agreement. Jack threw a good evening to them over his shoulder and climbed into his vehicle. He knew they were worried for Dulcie, but he had no intention to give them a reason to fear.

Chapter Three

Dulcie looked at herself in the vanity mirror one last time. Her hair was up in a casual but pretty style that allowed curls to tumble down her neck and tendrils to frame her face. Her hands shook as she raised the double strands of white pearls forming a collar style necklace to encircle her throat. That was it. The last piece was in place. All she had left to do was go down stairs and join her family.

So why couldn't she move? She had had dinner with Jackson many times before. Tonight was exactly the same. Her family would be present, as always. Dulcie cheeks flushed as her conscience reminded her why it was different. Jackson had kissed her. He had touched her. Intimately. Her nipples hardened and her breath left her in a rush just at the memory. She picked up the dance card from the night before and opened it to see Jackson's name written in his masculine yet elegant script on every line.

A gentle knock clicked against the door. "Miss?"

"Yes, Oliver?"

"The Duke and Duchess and the Marquess are waiting for you, milady."

"Please inform them I will be down shortly." Dulcie straightened the items on her vanity. The silver handle of her hairbrush was cold and she picked up the object, hoping to cool her sweating palms. Another knock and she replaced the brush and rose from the vanity bench. "I said I would be down shortly, Oliver."

Dulcie marched to the door and threw it open only to be confronted with the ever handsome Jackson. "What...What... What...?"

"You are taking a very long time getting ready, my dear. I thought I would come see if there was any way I could help."

Jackson stepped into her bedroom, closing the door behind him. Dulcie's heart stopped beating.

"N-no, no, Jackson. There is nothing you can do.... What are you doing?" Dulcie asked breathlessly. She was backed up against the side of her bed. Jackson stood directly in front of her, the toes of his highly polished boots brushing the hem of her green silk dress.

When he stepped those last few inches forward, Dulcie felt her body dissolve. His hands skimmed up her back, his fingertips tickled her neck. He reached her hair and began plucking out the carefully arranged pins. "I want to see your hair down tonight, darling."

"All right," she breathed. As her hair fell in long spiraling curls, Dulcie watched Jackson's face. He paid careful attention to his task, obviously afraid he might hurt her. His fingers felt wonderful as they threaded through her hair. She sighed as she leaned into him. Her hands rose to his chest and flattened her palms against the wool of his dinner jacket. The dark grey material felt cool beneath her fingers as she swept them back and forth. Even through the heavy material, however, she could feel the erratic beating of his heart. It matched hers.

When he finished arranging her hair around her shoulders, he looked into her eyes and smiled softly. "You are so very beautiful, Dulcie."

"You make me feel so, Jackson."

"Call me Jack."

Dulcie smiled. "Say please," she taunted softly. She didn't know where this sultry seductress had come from but she hoped she stayed.

Jackson gently but firmly gripped the back of her head and pulled her close to his lips. "Please."

"Jack," she whispered.

Jackson kissed her, his tongue going deep, brushing against her tongue, engaging her. Dulcie sighed, following his movements as though it were a dance. It was a dance she wanted to continue, especially when his hand came between them to cup her breast. *Her breast!* She remembered the wondrous feelings he had created the last time he touched her there. She remembered what he said he would do if they hadn't been at that soiree with all of those other people. Dulcie leaned away, breaking their kiss.

Jackson merely rubbed and pinched her pebbled nipple. He made no move to pull her flesh into his mouth. It was very frustrating. He teased her flesh and, by the smile on his face, he knew it.

"Jackson—"

"Jack," he corrected in his husky, intimate voice.

"Jack," she said breathily. "Please. Kiss me."

"Where, darling?"

"There," she said.

"There?" Jackson asked.

"There, Jack. Down... there. Please," she begged softly as he pinched and twisted gently.

Jackson smiled and bore her back against her bed. "It would be my utmost pleasure to kiss you... down there, darling," he whispered before taking her lips again. This time his kiss was slow, still deep, but not fast and uncontrolled like before. His previous kiss had been like a thunderstorm, in like a flash, loud, shaking, and frightening. This kiss was like the fog. It was slow and thick, it found every nook and filled it as if with mist and mystery and made everything seem like a dream.

She was light-headed when Jackson pulled back. He kissed her just beneath her bottom lip. He kissed her chin and the soft flesh underneath, her throat, the center of her collarbone. He kissed her breastbone above the bodice of her dress, kissed the silk outline of each distended nipple. Dulcie didn't realize what Jackson was doing with his hands until she felt her legs being pressed wide open. "Jack, wait," she said weakly.

"Just one taste, darling. I promise on your heart and soul I will not do more than kiss you."

When Dulcie felt the first touch of Jackson's fingers in the cluster of auburn curls at the top of her thighs, all of the stiffness left her body. She didn't understand. It was as though his touch produced a drug her body responded to immediately; as though laudanum seeped from his pores into hers.

His fingertips sifted through the curls and edged along the seam of her sex. When he pulled her open, it was a strange sensation. Cool air touched the hot wet flesh but she wasn't exposed to it for long. Dulcie let out a soft cry when Jackson's lips touched her sex. They were soon followed by his tongue. The pointed tip circled then traveled up to the front of her sex, where it found the most painfully sensitive piece of flesh she had never realized existed. She couldn't prevent how her hips bucked when he flicked the spot with his tongue.

Jackson lifted his mouth. "No, no, no," Dulcie begged quietly.

"Shh, darling. Do you know how delicious you are? How exquisite you are? How could I stop?" Jackson lowered his face back to her sex and flicked his tongue against that spot again. "This is your clit, darling. It is a most beautiful knot of feeling, isn't it?"

"Yes," Dulcie replied, drawing it out in a hiss.

"And here," Jackson said as his tongue moved lower, "is where I will claim you on our wedding night." Jackson's tongue slid in slow and deep and Dulcie groaned. He repeated the motion two, three more times before pulling away and looking into her eyes over the length of her body. "There is a piece of flesh in there we will break on that night. Tonight, right now, we will practice making you feel so very good you will not notice when I break it."

With a wicked smile, Jackson's mouth returned to her clit and Dulcie buried her fingers in his hair. The feeling was so sharp and pleasurable, tears crowded her vision. His tongue circled and flicked while he suckled on the nub. When she felt one of his fingers circle her opening in time to his tongue circling her clit, her entire body rocked and shuddered.

Dulcie would have cried out loud had Jackson not pushed himself up at the last moment and covered her mouth with his. His lips tasted salty and sweet. It was a strange flavor though not unpleasant. He didn't pull away until her body had stopped shaking. "How do you feel?" He asked.

"I've never felt anything like it."

Jackson chuckled and she felt it rumble through her body. "Is that good or bad, Dulcie?"

"Good, Jack. Very good," she replied quietly. Dulcie could feel her cheeks heat.

Jackson tipped her chin up, not an easy task as they were still lying on her bed, until she looked at him. "I'm glad for it then. We will make each other happy, Dulcie. I know we will."

Dulcie had no doubt Jackson would make her happy. She had been half in love with her friend all her life. However, she knew she did not compare to the bright, shining, petite beauties so popular among the ton. She wondered if she really could make Jackson happy or if he was settling for some reason that completely escaped her.

Chapter Four

Dulcie again smoothed the emerald silk over her thighs. It was ridiculous. She knew her dress was in perfect order, but she couldn't help remembering the skirt around her waist. Nor could she forget Jackson's face between her thighs, his mouth delivering the most incredible sensation in the world.

"Are you all right, Pixie?"

Dulcie looked up to find her mother staring at her with concern. "Yes, Mother, why?"

"You haven't touched your food," the duchess replied. "And you look a tad piqued. Are you certain you are all right?"

Dulcie laughed and picked up her fork. "Yes, yes, I'm fine. See?" Dulcie made a grand show of taking several bites of the delicious veal dinner.

Her mother smiled and turned her attention to Dulcie's father. Dulcie let her gaze drift to Jackson. He was watching her intently. When she raised her head and looked him square in the eye, his lips curled into a secretive smile that turned her bones to water.

For the rest of the evening, every time she looked at him, the same smile creased his mouth. He even had the nerve to wink at her! She had to hide her blush, and her smile, behind her napkin. If Jackson didn't stop soon, Dulcie was certain her face would be red forever.

After dinner, Jackson asked permission to take Dulcie out to the garden for a stroll. Her father looked suspiciously at Jackson but nodded and called for Oliver to get a shawl for Dulcie. With the velvet and lace wrapped around her shoulders, Jackson escorted her out onto the terrace and to the garden path dappled with moonlight.

The heady scents of late blooming flowers surrounded them. Jackson didn't touch her but stayed close to her side. Dulcie moved to pass a large topiary but Jackson's arm wrapped around her waist and pulled her behind the large, shaped bush. Dulcie looked up into his eyes.

The smile on his face now, here in the quiet and intimacy of the garden, was warm and, dare she hope, loving. "Ah, Dulcie."

"Hmm?"

"I am thinking of how happy we will be when we are wed," he murmured.

Dulcie bit her lip and smiled. "Have I said I would marry you, Jackson?"

Jackson growled in response to her playfulness. They both knew she would marry him. "Should I remind you of one of the reasons *why* you should marry me?" Cool air touched her calves and she realized Jackson was raising her dress.

"Cornell! What do you think you're doing? We are outside!" Dulcie batted his hands away from her and jumped away. She smoothed her hands over her plump bottom, grimacing a little as she did. It was still hard for her to believe that Jackson would choose her above all others. She looked up and was intrigued by the look on his face. It was one she had seen before between her parents and her siblings and their spouses. It was a look of desire tempered by affection. Perhaps Jackson saw something she did not when she looked in the mirror.

"Come here," Jackson commanded.

Deciding she felt like being contrary Dulcie replied, "No."

One thick black eyebrow lifted. "I said come here, Dulcie."

She cleared her throat and stiffened her spine. "No."

Jackson stepped away from the topiary with a growl. Dulcie yelped and turned. She dashed through the garden, around now-headless rose bushes, even jumping over very low flowers. Jackson laughed behind her and Dulcie giggled in response. He caught her just before she reached the terrace and pulled her into the shadows created by a niche between two tall conifers and the townhouse.

"No more playing tonight, hmm?" Jackson asked. His voice was husky and breathless. It made Dulcie shiver with a longing she wouldn't have understood only a few days, perhaps even a few hours ago.

"I... I don't know how much more of you're playing I can take, Jackson," she whispered in reply.

"Let us find out." Jackson's head dipped to hers. His lips skimmed over her eyebrow, across her cheekbone, down her nose. He nipped the tip and Dulcie whimpered. She couldn't see his face, but knew he was smiling at her, damn him. His lips touched hers. And damn her, too, if that was where she had to go to receive more of his wonderful kisses and caresses.

Jackson's tongue slipped into her mouth and Dulcie sighed, sifting her fingers deep into his hair. His movements were soft and slow and she couldn't take it. She needed fire and passion. Dulcie aggressively brushed his tongue with hers. She breeched his mouth and explored all she could. His flavor was even stronger inside. Dulcie tried to get closer.

Jackson's hands moved restlessly over her body. One moment they pressed into her back, the next they circled to her front to cup her breasts. When her nipples stood hard and aching, he left them. Cool air once again hit her legs as he raised her skirt. She didn't care. When the silk was gathered around her hips, he wedged his thigh high between hers.

Jackson's mouth left hers. "Spread your legs for me, love."

When she did, his hard leg connected with her delicate sex, her sensitive clit. The raw silk material of his trousers chafed the nub directly. Dulcie gasped. Jackson's mouth returned to hers. Jackson kissed her hard and deep, stealing her breath as he guided her with his hands on her hips, shifting them. Back and forth, she rode his thigh.

Her chest seized as her body shuddered and the muscles deep inside of her contracted. Dulcie laid her forehead against Jackson's shoulder. "Dulcie," he said in a strained voice.

"Yes?'

"Forgive me."

"For what," she asked. His answer was to surge his hips against her belly, time and time again until he groaned her name. He shivered against her and Dulcie held him tight, wishing she could see Jackson's face.

Jackson's erratic breathing stirred the hair at her temple. "I shouldn't have done that," he whispered.

"Why not?" She tried to pull back so that she could look up into his face but he wouldn't allow it. He moved one hand to the small of her back, the other up to cradle the back of her head. The feel of his arms around her, holding her close, was so heavenly. Dulcie wrapped her arms around Jackson's waist and sighed. If this was how they would stay until he answered her, she could wait.

Insects chirped around them, leaves rustled, their breathing and heartbeats slowed. Dulcie was content to listen to it all. Unfortunately, the cold painfully pricked the skin of her legs and she shivered. Jackson removed his leg and laughed softly when she tightened her thighs, trying to stop him. They worked her skirt back into place and though her legs were no longer cold, she missed the contact with his body.

His hands smoothed her hair back from her face and cupped her cheeks. She looked up, able to make out his features thanks to the moonlight illuminating the strong lines. "I should have waited," he said. "I should have waited until I can be inside of you, fill you with my flesh." He looked up and stepped away, pulling her with him from the shadows. "In private."

"Dulcie? Jackson?" Her mother came out onto the terrace and approached the marble balustrade. "I'm sorry, Jackson. The duke isn't feeling terribly well. He apologizes for cutting the evening short, but he thinks it best..." her mother trailed off, too polite to ask a guest to leave.

"Of course, my Lady," Jackson said with a half bow to the duchess. He led Dulcie back inside and she decided it was time to retire for the evening. As they passed her, she kissed her mother's cheek and wished her a good night.

Her father, his complexion pale, sat before the fireplace in the study. She kissed the top of his head. "Good night, Papa."

"Good night, my dear." Jackson made to follow her from the room into the hallway but her father stopped him. "Jack, please, stay for a few moments."

Dulcie looked up into his eyes. "Good night, Jackson."

"Jack," he murmured intimately.

"Good night, Jack," she said with a small smile.

"Good night, Dulcie." He lifted her hand to his lips, but instead of kissing her knuckles, he kissed her palm.

Closing her fingers in to capture his caress, Dulcie hurried up to her room for a night of glorious dreams and fitful sleep.

* * *

Jack watched until the last bit of Dulcie's dress was no longer visible before turning back to her parents. The smile faded from his face when he saw the stern expressions on theirs. Lord Abraham started to talk but a coughing fit overtook him and Jack hurried to get the older man a drink of water. When he was comfortable, Lord Abraham started again.

"You were upstairs for a long time earlier, Jack."

"Yes," he saw no point in denying it. The man could easily tell time.

Lord Abraham looked at him for a moment before rubbing the skin at either side of his mouth. Lady Moira made a disgusted noise in her throat. "Abe!"

"Ahem. Look, I expect you to behave yourself, Jack. Is that clear?"

"Yes, Your Grace."

"Good. Now then, my other children and their wives and husband are going to the Tower tomorrow." The duke pulled a handkerchief to his mouth and coughed.

His wife went to him and rubbed his back as she spoke to Jack. "You can meet them at eleven in the morning and you and Dulcie will stay with them and in sight at all times."

"Of course, my Lady," Jack assented. It took everything within him not to smile. He did not want his future mother-in-law to think he was mocking her. He just knew that nothing would stop him from finding even one moment alone with Dulcie. However, he would never, ever hurt her. "I would never do anything to embarrass Dulcie in public, Lady Moira, rest assured. I respect and admire her too much."

The duchess nodded her approval. "Thank you." The duke's coughing grew louder. "Oh dear. Jack, if you wouldn't mind showing yourself out, I need Oliver to take my husband to bed." She called for the butler and instructed the man to move the duke to his room immediately.

Not wanting to interrupt the delicate moment, Jack left the room, pulled on his wool jacket and hat, and left the residence. His coach pulled up in front of the house but he couldn't help looking back one last time. In the front right window was Dulcie's curvaceous outline. A smile tipped his lips as he swept off his hat and performed a full court bow. When he looked back, Dulcie's hand rested on the window, as if reaching out to him. He touched his fingers to his lips and blew her a kiss before climbing into his coach.

Chapter Five

Dulcie gripped her hands tightly, willing herself not to move the curtain and look ahead for Jackson. There would be too many people and they were still to far away to see him, she reminded herself. She forced her hands apart, skimmed them over the fine, fluttery material of her pink morning dress and adjusted the bottom and cuffs of her Spencer jacket.

"Dulcie, dear, stop fidgeting," Arian said.

Reagan took Dulcie's left hand in both of her smaller ones. "You look perfect."

"He won't be looking at anything but you," Elaine predicted. They were all quiet for a moment then her sister said, "We are all going to be keeping close eyes on the two of you. The men especially, I am sure. Mama is suspicious that something... improper may have transpired in your bedroom last night."

Though she tried desperately not to think on it, Dulcie's cheeks heated. A shadow of feeling tugged at her clit as she remembered the way Jackson had licked and sucked on her. The other women burst into fits of giggles which only made Dulcie blush more. Reagan and Arian begged to know what happened while Elaine begged her to remain silent. Dulcie didn't think she could ever speak of the things she and Jackson had done in her room. She just wanted to do them again. And find out what else they could do together.

The carriage drew to a stop and they waited as the coachman opened the door. Her brothers, brother-in-law, and Jackson were all waiting for them. She noticed Jackson was straightening his clothing and that his hair had been mussed. Growling in annoyance, she stepped down first to help Arian. Miles rushed forward to assist them. Under her breath, she spat at her brother, "We will be having a discussion later on how to treat long standing family friends."

Miles had the gall to smile as he said, "We know how to treat them, Pixie. That's why he isn't swimming in the Thames." Once her pregnant sister-in-law was safely on the ground, Dulcie punched Miles in the arm.

She walked to Jackson who was smoothing his hair back into place. A rueful smile split his face and Dulcie shook her head. "I am sorry for them."

"Don't be. It warms my heart to know my bride-to-be is so well protected." He kept his voice low but light.

A blush heated her cheeks and she broke eye contact. "You keep saying things like that and I will expect a wedding sooner or later."

"It is a promise I make and intend to keep, Dulcie. Do not question that." She looked up through her lashes. His expression was serious but gentle and her heart melted anew. Jackson leaned forward and Dulcie turned her face up to his. Just as his lips were about to touch hers, someone to her very immediate left cleared his throat.

William stood so close his chest brushed against her sleeve. "I believe we should be getting inside now. Everyone stay close, we wouldn't want to lose anyone." Her brother inserted himself between Dulcie and Jackson as the group walked to the building that housed so many treasures, everything from royal to natural.

She bent back a little as she walked and looked at Jackson. He was watching her and when she caught his gaze, he winked. The twinkle in his eyes told her he had something on his mind. Something that made her blush.

Try as they did, however, there was no evading the men of her family. One always seemed to be at her side. There was never an opportunity for a private moment with Jackson and after what she had experienced at his hand it was frustrating not to be able to feel those sensations again. When they left the Tower and bid Jackson good evening, he took a chance. Though her brothers were close at hand and they stood outside for all to see, Jackson took Dulcie in his arms and kissed her deeply.

He released her and tipped his hat to her family, disappearing into the crowd before her brothers and brother-in-law could extricate themselves from their wives to go after him. Dulcie watched after him even though she couldn't see him for long after he left her side. Smiling to herself, Dulcie climbed into the carriage.

Daniel stuck his head into the vehicle and smiled at the women. "We are just going to go catch up with Jack and see if he wants to go to the club for a drink."

"You three will do nothing of the sort," Dulcie said slowly.

William leaned in around their brother-in-law. "It's just a friendly drink, Pixie."

"That's right!" Miles contributed.

"I don't want you three harassing him anymore. Jackson isn't hurting me and, though I do not wish to get ahead of myself, he has been speaking of marriage to me. So, as much as I love the three of you, if you hurt him, I will wreak havoc upon you. Understand?" Dulcie looked between the three men.

"Marriage?" William asked.

"Yes."

Comically, the trio turned as one to look in the direction Jackson had disappeared. They turned to each other and nodded before looking back to Dulcie. "We'll leave him be. For now," William promised her.

Knowing it was the best she would be able to extract from them, Dulcie smiled her gratitude. Just before Miles closed the door, Arian said to him, "We need to stop by Madame Elise's to pick up our dresses for tomorrow night's ball at the Duke of Chelsey's."

Miles took his wife's hand and kissed her knuckles lingeringly. Dulcie could see the love between her brother and his wife and wondered if she and Jackson would have that; if they could build on their attraction and tenderness to an enduring lifetime of love. If not, she wondered if her love for him, the love she had never realized was so strong, would be enough.

"Dulcie?" Elaine placed her hand on Dulcie's arm and squeezed gently.

"Hmm?" She turned to her sister who was looking at her with concern.

"Are you all right? You drifted away from us," Elaine said.

Dulcie laughed, shaking her head, scattering her questions to ponder later. "Yes, I apologize. I was merely thinking of... something." When the other women asked her to elaborate she declined. The others groaned good-naturedly and Dulcie laughed.

She didn't want to admit she had doubts about her future with Jackson, she only hoped those fears were unfounded.

Chapter Six

Dulcie and her mother entered the ball room of the Duke of Chelsey's London home. Her heart stopped at the sight of Jackson standing at the bottom of the stairs. He was smiling up at her with open tenderness and desire. His immaculate evening wear was so far from his norm it made Dulcie feel very special to think he may have dressed so for her. As she came to stand before him, Jackson gave her a very proper bow and took her hand in his.

He kissed her knuckles before tucking her hand in the bend of his elbow. Jackson offered his other arm to her mother then returned his full attention to her. "You look beautiful, Dulcie."

Heat stung her cheeks but she was very happy he was so pleased by her appearance. "Thank you, Jackson. You look very nice tonight, too."

Jackson grinned down at her and led the two women further into the room. He gently rubbed her fingers, letting his slide between hers. Dulcie shivered at the intimate sensation. She shivered as she again thought of what those fingers could do. Her inner thighs grew damp and she blushed.

They found Arian who was sitting out most of the dances due to her pregnancy. Lady Moira released Jackson's arm and sat with her daughter-in-law. After bowing to the women, Jackson turned to Dulcie and, with a wicked smile on his handsome face, said, "I have yet again claimed all of your dances for myself."

Dulcie blushed as Jackson led her out onto the ballroom floor. She knew he likely had no competition, but that he would imply that he did made her practically giddy. On the parquet, Jackson took her in his arms and they moved in practiced steps to the music. His strong arms told her where he wanted her to go and she followed blindly. The music changed and with it the dance. Dulcie sighed as she and Jackson were made to separate and not be as close as the waltz allowed.

Two lines formed on either side of the ballroom. It was the first time that night she saw Caressa, who waved her over to stand next to her in line. They were not far from the front, being daughters of Dukes. Lord Chelsey and his betrothed stood at the head of either line. As the pair began their progression, everyone laughed and cheered.

Caressa nudged Dulcie with her elbow. "I see Jackson is being very attentive, as he was at the last ball. Tell me, is something happening between the two of you?"

Dulcie felt herself blush. "Jackson has made his intentions known," she said to her friend in a whisper.

A beatific smile spread across the smaller woman's face. "And what does he intend?"

"He has spoken of... a future," Dulcie provided evasively.

"Oh!" Caress squealed, hugging Dulcie's arm tightly. "I am so happy for you, Dulcie." She looked across the dance floor. When Jackson moved his eyes from Dulcie to Caressa, the small woman smiled and clapped her hands at him. Jackson smiled and bowed slightly, acknowledging her friend's praise.

As they progressed to the front of the line, Dulcie smoothed the apple green silk of her skirt, wondering if she and Jackson would find time to themselves tonight. Caressa and her dance partner walked a short way down the aisle created by the rows of people. When they began to dance, Dulcie laughed and clapped for her friend. She looked across to Jackson who was smiling at her with not a small amount of heat shining in his eyes. Unable not to fidget, Dulcie adjusted her white satin gloves, the tops of which came half way up her upper arms.

Caressa and her partner made it to the end of the aisle and Jackson stepped into the middle, holding his hand out to Dulcie. Taking a deep breath, she stepped forward and placed her hand in his. Their contemporaries were not used to seeing Dulcie on the dance floor over much. In the country dance, everyone could see you, everyone watched. She allowed Jackson to lead her past the first few pairs of dancers before he took her back into the circle of his arms and waltzed her to the end. Though it was a dance they had all been taking part in only moments ago, the two of them dancing it alone in front of everyone could be considered shocking.

She heard several scandalized indrawn breaths and murmurs from the women's side. From the men's side came low chuckles, words of encouragement to Jackson, and, if she wasn't mistaken, two threats on his life. She had no doubt from who they were and laughed at William and Daniel.

At the end of the aisle, Jackson kissed the palm of her hand before releasing her. When she went back to standing next to Caressa, the smaller woman giggled into her hand. "That was quite the show, dear. You had best watch out or there will be talk of a different nature before the night is through."

Dulcie, who had always concerned herself with propriety, didn't much care what the *ton* thought of her dance with Jackson. All she cared about was how Jackson made her feel. How he touched her. "I do not care."

She looked down at Caressa who was staring at her as if she had never before seen Dulcie. It didn't sound like her, she knew, but it was the truth. "Well, then," Caressa said, "I...I... I don't know what to say except I am happy for you." The expression on her friend's face was one of confusion but she still wore her happy, sparkling smile.

Dulcie stared across the dance floor at Jackson. He watched her in return, his lips curled in that devilish smile she had come to love. Caressa sighed next to her. "He looks positively taken with you."

"I certainly hope so," Dulcie said quietly.

As the dance came to an end, couples came together again as a reel began to play. Jackson appeared at her side, his hand at the small of her back. "Come with me," he whispered in her ear.

They made their way to the rear of the room where French doors led to the veranda. Once outside, Jackson took her hand and hurried down the side of the duke's home. They came upon the doors to the duke's library which stood slightly ajar. Jackson guided her inside, closing the French doors behind them.

"Beautiful, beautiful Dulcie," Jackson murmured, pulling her into his arms. His lips touched hers and Dulcie grabbed hold of his shoulders, kissing him back with all the fervor he gave.

Jackson walked her backwards and turned. Something hit the backs of her knees and he pressed her shoulders for her to sit. He bent forward and lifted her hands to his lips before standing upright and holding her open palms to his chest. Guiding her hands with his, Jackson trailed them down the front of his body. "I need you to touch me, Dulcie. Don't be afraid, darling, please. I just need to feel you."

Their hands came to rest against the front of his trousers and he molded her fingers around a long, thick bulge. He squeezed her fingers and groaned, his head falling back. Dulcie felt her sex grow wetter than before and moved her hands along his hardness. She squeezed gently, using the same amount of pressure he had. Jackson groaned, his hands falling away from hers.

His hips began to sway from side to side against the motions of her hands. Jackson jerked away from her and unfastened the buttons of his pants. "Take off your gloves, love."

Dulcie didn't question his thick-voiced command, merely pulled the slick material down her arms and dropped them on the floor. She watched Jackson shove his trousers partway down his thighs and when he stood up straight his sex was at her eye level. The end was dark pink and shaped like a plum, large, smooth and round with a cleft along the top. The shaft was long and thickest in the middle and had blue lines tracing under the skin. A large sack hugged tight to the base. She had never seen anything quite like it and while it frightened her, she also could not stop herself from reaching out to touch him.

Jackson sucked in a breath then released a harsh groan. She looked up and his eyes bored into hers. He licked his lips. His fingers touched her cheek. "I know... I know this may scare you, but, please, kiss me."

Dulcie smiled and stretched up to press her lips to his. Jackson shook his head. "No, kiss my cock. Remember how I kissed you in your bedroom?" Dulcie swallowed and nodded. He smiled and she knew he was trying to be gentle as his voice softened. "Please, kiss me like that. Take me into your mouth."

Dulcie looked at the organ in her hand. It seemed impossible that she would be able to take much of him inside but she leaned forward, placing a gentle kiss on the tip before opening her mouth for him. The taste of his skin was intoxicating and she lapped at the head. Her teeth scraped against him and he hissed softly. Afraid she had hurt him, she curled her lips over her teeth to protect him.

"Ah, yes, Dulcie." Jackson's voice was shaky as were his hands as they touched her face, her neck. He tore the pins from her hair and delved his fingers into the heavy mass. "Suck, love."

She did as he asked and his hands guided her head away and forward, over and over. Dulcie took the lead and moved on her own, sucking and licking. Moans and groans left Jackson's mouth in a constant stream until he pulled out of her mouth and turned away from her. He pulled his cravat from around his neck but she couldn't see what he was doing. The tight globes of his rear and the ropes of muscle along his thighs convulsed again and again.

When he turned back to her, Dulcie could see his *cock*, as he had called it, was softening and shrinking. Jackson tossed his balled cravat on the floor with her gloves and knelt down in front of her, wedging his way between her legs. He cupped her jaw and kissed her hard and deep. Dulcie dissolved into the kiss.

She felt Jackson's hands move to her shoulders and push the sleeves of her dress and the straps of her half corset down her arms. He continued until he had uncovered her breasts. They spilled out of the silk and cotton and Jackson pulled back to look at them. "What a beautiful sight," he said and leaned down to press his firm lips to the peaks.

Dulcie's fingers inched the hem of her skirt up her legs until she could spread her thighs wider. Jackson looked down then back up to her face, his wicked smile again curling his lips. "Now that is a sight worthy of worship."

Dulcie blushed and pulled his head close again. This time, Jackson opened his mouth and sucked her nipple into his mouth. Dulcie sighed and gasped. The sensation seemed to go straight through her down to her core.

Jackson's fingers glided up Dulcie's leg and she shivered. He traveled his way up the inside of her thigh straight to her weeping center. Dulcie couldn't contain the squeal that left her lips as he pressed his fingers as deep as he could into her sheath. "So hot and wet, my darling Dulcie. I can hardly wait until we are wed."

Dulcie couldn't reply as he began thrusting his fingers in and out in a pleasure inducing rhythm. His lips returned to her breast and he suckled on her. Dulcie grabbed a hold of the back of his head and curved her back, offering him all she had. When her climax came over her, Dulcie cried out her lover's name, her eyes squeezed shut as ecstasy rolled through her. When she returned to earth, Dulcie opened her eyes to smile at Jackson.

The vision before her was not one she wanted to see during a clandestine meeting with Jackson. The hallway door to the library stood open. In the doorway were a gaping Duke of Chelsey, his betrothed, and many of their guests, including one man who stood laughing and clapping.

The man who had once claimed to love her and had offered for her, the shining Baron Frederick Bartel pointed and laughed. "Had I known you could be that much fun, Dulcie, perhaps I'd have gone through with the marriage!"

Jackson pulled away from her and turned to rush the baron. Her brothers were on him before he made it far, however. William tackled Jackson to the floor. Miles knelt beside the two, punching Jackson anywhere he could reach. Daniel fell on the pack, holding Jackson's arms as he tried to defend himself.

Dulcie didn't know how long she sat there with her skirt pulled up and her bodice pulled down. She finally came to and fixed her clothing as she rushed to Jackson's aid. "Get off of him! William, Miles, leave him be! Daniel, let go of his arms!"

She jumped into the fray and her brothers stopped immediately, likely afraid they would hurt her. None would look at her as they wheeled away from her and Jackson. A red lap blanket was draped across a wingback chair that was within reach and she grabbed it, laying it over Jackson's exposed lap. She cradled his head in her lap, noting the bruises already forming on his face.

The Baron walked over and knelt on one knee beside her. He picked up a lock of her hair. "Seeing as how your current *suitor*," he said snidely, "is incapacitated, perhaps you would care to join me in one of the guest bedrooms?"

Dulcie saw red as she turned to look at the man she had thought she loved all those years ago during her first season when she was seventeen. Her brain hadn't even completed the thought before her knuckles slammed into his perfect nose. The baron fell backwards, clutching his nose. "You stupid bitch!"

"I was once," she agreed, referring to when she had agreed to marry him seven years ago. "I am not anymore. Come near me again and suffer the consequences."

She looked down at Jackson who smiled up at her from her lap. "I believe I am supposed to defend your honor."

"And how do you propose to do that in your current state?" Dulcie asked gently, smoothing his hair from his forehead.

"She has no honor left to protect, thanks to you," William said from behind her. "Get up, Cornell."

Her oldest brother reached down and grabbed the front of Jackson's shirt. Dulcie tried to hold on to him, but Daniel held her arms. William and Miles dragged Jackson from the room. Dulcie's mother, whom Dulcie hadn't noticed among the crowd, walked up to her and said stiffly, "Come along, Dulcie. Your brothers are taking Jackson back to our townhouse. Let us go."

Dulcie could feel the displeasure and humiliation rolling off of her mother. She rose from the floor on shaky legs and was helped by Daniel outside and into their waiting carriage. The short trip home was excruciatingly quiet. Neither her mother nor her brother-in-law would look at her.

When they reached their destination and walked into the house, Dulcie could hear her father yelling. Her mother took her hand in a near painful grip and led her to her father's study. Inside, in one of the two chairs that faced her father's desk, sat Jackson. He was mussed and bloody. Dulcie sat in the chair next to his and reached for his hand.

Jackson looked at her and tried to smile. She squeezed his hand, grateful for the encouragement. She looked at her father who was staring out the window, taking deep breaths.

He was standing, which Dulcie knew was not a good thing. He wheezed and coughed into his hand. His entire body was shaking as he turned to look at Jackson and her.

"How could you, Jackson? How could you touch our daughter, in the middle of a party filled to the rafters with our friends and acquaintances?" Her father coughed again and shook his head. "She was an innocent girl and you've turned her into a...a—"

"Papa!"

"Well, it's true! We trusted you, Jackson. When Moira and I asked you to woo our Dulcie, we didn't ask you to molest her like she was some common trollop."

Her father's words turned her blood to ice. It froze in her veins as she heard her father's words over and over in her head. *When Moira and I asked you to woo our Dulcie.* They had asked him?

Dulcie felt Jackson's hand squeeze hers as he said her name. It was muffled as though he stood far away from her. "Dulcie?"

"You asked him to woo me?"

Everyone stopped and looked at Dulcie. She looked at Jackson. "Tell me it isn't true."

Jackson swallowed and looked from the duke to the duchess and back to Dulcie. "I cannot. But Dulcie, you have to believe—"

"No," she said, pulling her hand free of Jackson's. Her head felt shattered. This was a millions times worse than when the baron had betrayed her.

The way Jackson had spoken to her; the way he had held and touched her. She closed her eyes as a wave of nausea overcame her. "How could you?" Dulcie looked at her parents then at Jackson. "How could the three of you...?"

"Dulcie, let me explain," Jackson said.

But she couldn't. Dulcie ran from the room and up the stairs, slamming her bedroom door shut and locking herself inside. Jackson had never wanted her. Her parents had had to ask Jackson to woo her, no doubt to convince her to marry him. They went behind her back and arranged a match between her and Jackson. He had done his best to seduce her. The liberties she had allowed him to take made her stomach dip and she barely pulled out the chamber pot in time to wretch.

Chapter Seven

Dulcie crept across her bedroom floor one final time. She carefully placed her favorite books on top of the dresses she had stuffed into her traveling bag. She closed the large bag and pulled it off the bed, being careful not to let it crash onto the floor. It was barely five in the morning as she tiptoed from her room, down the stairs, and into the kitchen where the staff was already preparing breakfast.

"Good mornin', milady," said the head cook Polly, Oliver's wife.

"Good morning, Polly. Is Oliver here?"

"He's out back overseeing the gardeners and collecting flowers for the household." The short, thin woman smiled warmly and glanced down at Dulcie's bag.

"Thank you, Polly." Dulcie ran out the back door and found Oliver instructing one poor man in a tree which branches needed to be removed. "Oliver, I need some assistance."

The butler turned with a startled look on his face. He looked her over, his wise old eyes staying a few moments on the bag she carried. He looked back to her face and smiled. "Yes, miss, how can I be of service?"

Dulcie cleared her throat. "I am returning home to Rothshire early this season. Please have a carriage prepared." She reached into her bag, withdrawing a note she had addressed to her parents. "And give this to the duke and duchess when they come down for breakfast."

Oliver took the letter, looking with concern between her and the note. "Is everything all right, my lady?"

Dulcie forced a smile to her lips. "Of course. I just do not feel as though this Season has been productive and wish to return home."

Oliver bowed and went to have her transport made ready. Dulcie smiled to the gardener and went back into the house to wait. The kitchen buzzed with activity but Dulcie was not up to being around people. She asked Polly to prepare some food for her and the carriage driver so they may eat on the journey to her family's country estate. Once she was weighted down with the baskets, Dulcie left the kitchen and walked into the foyer.

As she passed, Dulcie looked into her father's office and was struck by visions of the night before. She heard her father's words, felt the tightening of her stomach, saw their blank, wide stares as she asked the question that had destroyed her.

After she had fled to her room, her mother and Jackson had followed her upstairs. They had banged on her door for an hour, her mother leaving first. Jackson had tried to cajole her into opening the door, had tried to threaten her into it. In the end there was one shuddering thud against the solid oak door and much cursing from Jackson. He had sworn to return, everyday, until she would speak to him. Through it all Dulcie had cried, her heart feeling as cold as ice.

The plan to leave had formed when the tears finally ran dry. She hadn't slept at all that night, staying awake and writing to her parents. The first dozen letters had been full of pain and rage and she had torn them all to shreds. A furious note would seem the act of a petulant child. She didn't want that. Dulcie wanted them to understand how much they had hurt her.

Her last note was simple. *I am returning home to Rothshire. There is no reason left to stay. Please do not return until after the end of the Season.*

A shudder wracked her body and she turned away, squeezing her eyes closed and breathing deeply. A hand landed lightly on her shoulder. "The carriage is ready, my lady."

Dulcie took one last deep breath and turned to bestow a smile on the butler. "Thank you, Oliver."

The faithful servant escorted her outside to the waiting transport and after helping her up, he cleared his throat. Dulcie looked at him expectantly. The words he spoke brought new tears to her eyes. "My lady, I would like to say that your parents love you very much and want only what is best for you. Nothing they may have done was meant to cause you pain."

"Thank you, Oliver, again. I merely need a little time to myself." Her throat was sore, her voice choked.

"Of course, my lady." Oliver bowed and closed the door. He instructed the carriage driver to move on and the still-quiet streets of London filled with the eerie sound of but two horses' hooves striking the cobblestones. Exhausted by her sleepless night, Dulcie laid the baskets of food and her one bag on the floor of the vehicle and turned sideways, lifting her legs to rest along the length of the seat.

With the exception of stopping to eat the lunch Polly had prepared, Dulcie slept the entire way to Rothshire. She was awoken by a hand gently jostling her shoulder. "My lady? My Lady Dulcie?"

She opened her eyes and yawned. Her dreams drifted away but she knew they had included Jackson. Her breathing and heartbeat were rapid and her thighs were slick. She had one fleeting vision of Jackson's fingers pumping into her before she ruthlessly burst it like a bubble in her mind.

The carriage driver helped her down and she thanked him as well as the skeleton staff who stood in the drive for her arrival. She told them she would not be down for dinner, she merely wished to rest until tomorrow. The two maids, cook, single footman, and the driver bowed to her as she walked into the manor house.

Rothshire was a beautiful house. It was large and full of light. It was home. Most importantly, at least for the moment, it was safe. Safe from the prying eyes of London, safe from her meddling parents as long as they stayed in London, and safe from one Jackson Cornell.

Chapter Eight

Jack's carriage pulled to a stop and he didn't wait for his driver to come down from his bench to open his door. He flung it open and jumped down onto the walk in front of the Duke of Rothshire's townhouse. He had received a message from the duke and his wife at half past eight in the morning. Twenty minutes later he was standing on their doorstep, pounding on the door.

When Oliver finally opened the door, Jack was close to kicking it open. "His Grace and the duchess are in the library."

Jack shouted his thanks as he moved past the man without even removing his hat and coat. He found them inside the book-lined room. The duchess paced the width of the room. The duke drummed a heavy staccato with his pencil against the tablet of paper resting on his lap. They both looked up but neither stopped, as though they were deep in thought and Jack was not a worthy distraction. He sat in a chair facing the duke, removing his hat respectfully.

"Where has she gone?" Jack asked quietly. The note in his pocket merely stated that Dulcie had left London.

"Dulcie has gone back to Rothshire," the duke said tiredly. "She has asked us to stay away. I cannot say that I blame her."

Jack swallowed roughly. His throat still ached from last night as he had stood outside Dulcie's bedroom, begging, challenging, threatening Dulcie. He had tried everything he could think of and his shoulder was still damn sore for it. None of it had done any good. He had left the hallway, the door still closed and locked. He had told her he would be back but she had fled before he could return.

He couldn't believe that she had left, slipping away in the wee hours of the morning to evade him. Now she was back in Rothshire, alone, giving her parents orders to stay away from her.

She is alone.

Jack's brain came back to that thought. Dulcie was back at her parents' estate, alone but for what was likely only a handful of household staff. No one was there. *No one to interfere.*

Jack cleared his throat, hoping he didn't sound giddy as he said, "If Dulcie wishes to be alone we must abide by her wishes."

"I cannot stand the thought of our little girl being so angry with us," the duchess said. She stopped her pacing so abruptly her skirts whipped around her ankles. Jack swallowed as she turned on him. "This is all your fault. If you had not touched our Dulcie in such a dishonorable manner she never would have learned of our arrangement."

Jack was sick with his own guilt, and he suspected her parents were as well, but he refused to allow the woman to try and place the blame solely on him. "Had you waited but a few days longer, I would have been on your doorstep, asking for Dulcie's hand myself." Jack didn't yell at her, but spoke quietly, hoping to make Dulcie's parents understand. "I should have come to you earlier, perhaps even years ago. I care deeply for your daughter and had made up my mind long ago to have her for my wife."

Lady Moira sobbed once and turned away. Lord Abraham sighed and coughed into his handkerchief. "Why didn't you tell us, son?"

"You gave my pride a reason to remain silent of my feelings for her. Now, she has left and we are all to blame." Jack felt he owed them that truth before he lied to them. "I think it would be best if we gave Dulcie the time and space she needs."

Her parents nodded their agreement. Jack apologized for his actions at the Duke of Wesley's soiree and left. He told his driver to get him home as quickly as possible. There, Jack ordered several bags packed as he hurried to his office.

Jack sat at his desk and pulled a key from his vest pocket. In the bottom drawer of his desk was a simple white birch box, small versions of their family crests carved in the front. The initials DNB were carved in an elegant scroll on the top. Dulcie Nan Brighton. Jack brushed his fingers across the letters before unlocking the box and lifting the lid. Inside was every trinket he had bought for Dulcie and had never had the courage to give to her. Earbobs, hair pins, bracelets, necklaces,...a ring.

The ring was the last object he'd acquired. A large emerald cut diamond in a white gold setting. It was pure and clean, understated but beautiful, just like his Dulcie. And she was his. In a few hours she would know.

*   *   *

Dulcie heard the hoof beats but thought nothing of them. She had sent one of the cook's sons into the village of Rothshire to acquire some of the freesia scented soap and oil she enjoyed using in her baths. Those items had been left behind in her hurry to leave London.

She grew suspicious when heavy knocking sounded at the door. The cook's son would have ridden to the back of the house and entered the kitchen, leaving the items for her with his mother. She saw the footman, Neil, hurry past the salon door. The deep smooth voice she heard was not a welcome one. He was too far away for her to hear his conversation with Neil, but the voice could not be mistaken.

Dulcie had just risen from the chaise, intending to close and lock the door before Jackson could find his way to her. Unfortunately, Jackson moved faster than she did. He was standing in the portal before she was half way to the door. "Hello, darling."

His rich voice spouting the false endearment made her heart kick inside of her chest. "What are you doing here?" Dulcie had intended for her voice to sound unaffected and strong. Instead it came out in the barest whisper.

Dulcie backed away as Jackson came into the room. He didn't stop until Dulcie had herself pressed against the pink silk covered wall. Raising a hand, Jackson gently cupped her chin. "It seems that you have misunderstood a great many things, love. I am here to set you straight."

Dulcie sputtered indignantly but Jackson ignored her. He moved into her stance until Dulcie was certain not even air could pass between them. "You will marry me, Dulcie. And it will have nothing to do with your parents or any obligation I may feel."

Jackson placed his free hand against her chest, just above her erratically beating heart. "It will have everything to do with this," he tapped his finger once. "And this." Dulcie gasped as Jackson pressed his lips against hers. He didn't try to force her mouth to open or make her take his tongue inside. The simple kiss was filled with purity and emotion.

Jackson pulled away and looked down into her eyes. Dulcie felt disoriented as she looked into his earnest hazel eyes. *No!* She shook her head to clear it. She would not fall for his lies and deceptions again. Pushing against his shoulders, Dulcie scrambled away from him.

"Leave this very moment, Cornell."

"No," Jackson replied, straightening his jacket and tugging his cuffs.

Dulcie shook with anger. "What?"

"I said, no." He looked over her shoulder. "Ah, Neil, when my carriage arrives from London, please place my things in the room across from Lady Dulcie's."

Dulcie whirled and looked at the footman. "Do nothing of the sort, Neil."

Not having heard him move, Dulcie jumped when Jackson's hands came down on her shoulders and he nuzzled her nape. "So, you would prefer they be placed in your bedroom?"

"Certainly not!" Dulcie exclaimed.

"The room across from Lady Dulcie's, Neil."

The man looked between the marquess and Dulcie five times before bowing out of the room, assuring Jackson it would be done. Jackson's fingers began to knead her tense shoulders and Dulcie tore herself away from the heavenly sensation. "Stay away from me, Cornell. I want you to leave in the morning. My concern isn't for you but for that poor horse you must have ridden so hard to get here. It is also for any misguided highwaymen who might have the misfortune of trying to steal from you. Wouldn't do for any of them to be heartbroken by the likes of you."

Dulcie immediately snapped her lips shut. She hadn't meant to say that aloud. She hadn't meant to let him know how terribly he had hurt her.

"Were you heartbroken, Dulcie?" His eyes looked remorseful. "It was not my intention to bring you pain, love."

"Intended or not." It was all she could say before tears clogged her throat. She would not cry in front of him; she needed to leave the room immediately. Dulcie turned her back on Jackson and left the salon. Once in the hallway, she dashed to the staircase and ran up to her room where she locked herself away. The tears came quickly. Humiliated tears, enraged tears, pained tears.

Dulcie could not believe he had followed her. How dare he! How would she live through his stay?

* * *

Jack watched Dulcie leave. When she was out of sight, he landed heavily on the settee. Her scent still lingered and his heart hurt. The pain in her eyes felt as though it just might kill him. He hated himself. All he had ever wanted was Dulcie and now she wouldn't come near him.

Neil appeared in the entrance of the room. Jack looked at the man who had condemnation written plainly on his face. The servant stepped into the room and, without concern that he was speaking to a nobleman, said, "I believe you should leave. I do not know what happened between you and my lady but the rest of the staff and I would prefer not to see her in such a state."

"It is my sincerest hope to make Dulcie smile again, Neil. I will not leave until that, at the very least, has been accomplished." Feeling the strength return to his legs, Jack got to his feet and made to leave the room.

Neil stepped into his path. "Perhaps she would smile if you would leave."

Jack smiled a little. It was truly a measure of how good a woman Dulcie was that so many loved and protected her. It was even a measure of her character, in his opinion, that so many of the *ton* treated her with such lack of appreciation. She was above them and they all knew it. And she treated her servants as though they were not beneath her. Dulcie was truly a rare creature and he loved her so much the thought of living without her nearly crippled him.

Jack patted the footman on the shoulder. "I'm afraid I cannot go without seeing a genuine smile for myself. If I were to leave, how would I see it?"

The man's nostrils flared but he allowed Jack to pass. Just outside the door, Jack bent down and retrieved his white birch box. He needed to rest. The stairs seemed to rise into Forever, but Jack dragged his tired body up and to the doorway of the room he requested. The pull to look across the hall was too much to resist.

He could hear the faint sounds of crying and his heart broke. He swore that whatever it took, he would never cause Dulcie to cry in sadness again. Tears of joy, he prayed for; tears of passion, he craved. But never again would she cry another tear in pain if he had his way.

Chapter Nine

Dulcie looked into the dining room and wanted to curse Jackson for the warmth that curled around her heart. The gas wall sconces were turned very low. Votive candles sprinkled light over one end of the long table. Jackson stood, in formal dinner attire, next to one of the high-backed chairs. He looked at her with a gentle smile.

Dulcie swallowed hard and entered the room. Jackson pulled out her chair. She didn't thank him as she sat. "You look lovely tonight, my Dulcie."

Her eyes and nose were red from crying, her hair sat atop her head in a sloppy knot, and the dress she wore was plain, brown, and several years out of fashion. If there was one word that would not describe her tonight, it would be lovely. "I am not your Dulcie."

Jackson rounded the end of the table and sat down across from her. "You will be," he replied cheerfully.

The maids served them roast beef with thick, fragrant gravy, yams, and asparagus. Once they poured Jackson some wine and Dulcie her favored cider, the maids retreated to the kitchen. "I shan't," Dulcie spat at him.

"We shall see." Jackson lifted his glass to her and took a healthy swallow before digging into his dinner with what looked to be ravenous hunger. Though he displayed impeccable manners, the speed with which he ate gave Dulcie a stomach ache.

She looked at her own plate. Though the food smelled wonderful, she did not have the appetite to eat it. Dulcie still couldn't believe Jackson was here at Rothshire. That he had followed her, as she tried to escape her humiliation at his hand, infuriated her. She felt like throwing her entire plate at his head.

When her hand seemed to work of its own volition to turn a spoonful of gravy and launch it like a trebuchet at Jackson's head,

Dulcie wasn't the least bit surprised. Dulcie looked across the table. She had always had wonderful aim. The gravy had landed square in the middle of Jackson's forehead. The look on his face was that of dumb shock.

For a moment, there was complete silence and stillness, the next, a slice of yam hit Dulcie in the chest. She gasped as the slick, buttery vegetable slid below her neckline. Dulcie picked up a dripping piece of beef and hurled it across the table. Food flew across the table. Jackson picked up the tureen full of asparagus; Dulcie lifted the silver gravy boat. Candles were extinguished until they were left in almost total dark.

Laughter and heavy breathing filled the room. Strong, slippery arms wrapped around her and brought her chest flush to Jackson's. His lips found her cheek first, finding his way to her mouth by feel. Gravy and butter was smeared across her face as Jackson opened his mouth over Dulcie's.

She gasped and Jackson's tongue thrust into her mouth. Dulcie's body reacted immediately. Her knees quivered as she grew hot and slick between her thighs. She couldn't let this happen, Dulcie knew. Jackson sucked on her lower lip as he pulled away to reposition his head.

The edge of the table came up against the backs of her thighs and Jackson pressed his pelvis against her belly. Dulcie felt light-headed. When Jackson's hands began pulling at her clothes and his lips left hers, Dulcie was dragging in deep, sobbing breaths.

"My beautiful Dulcie, I want to hear you cry out for me."

She would never cry for him again. Dulcie had promised that to herself that afternoon. Oh she knew that wasn't what he was asking for, but she would not give him the chance to break her again.

Dulcie pushed Jackson away, putting all of her strength into shoving his stronger body away from hers. His hands slipped from her gravy covered arms and Dulcie ran. Her right thigh caught the corner of the table and she stubbed her toe on the leg of the sideboard, but neither slowed her down. Nor did the stairs. Dulcie didn't stop until she made it to her bedroom.

She had to stay away from him. When he touched her, the room spun and she allowed him access to all parts of her body. That was no longer an option for them. Taking a steadying breath, Dulcie walked away from the door to go to her dressing room.

One look in the mirror had Dulcie falling to her knees, laughing so hard she could barely catch her breath. Her dress clung to her where gelatinous globs of gravy had soaked through the fabric. Her hair hung in heavy disgusting ropes around her. Her skin was smeared brown and yellow.

It took several minutes before Dulcie was able to pull herself together. She rung for a maid and asked for a bath to be prepared. With the dress covering most of her, the worst of the mess was confined to her hair, face, chest, and hands. After scrubbing bits of yam and beef, and pulling an asparagus spear from her hair, Dulcie rubbed a soapy cloth over her skin until she was pink. In the back of her mind she knew she was tying to scrub away the feel of Jackson's hands. She was trying to make herself forget.

It didn't work. When the slightly rough fabric brushed her nipples, she imagined it was Jackson's hands. Taking her freesia scented soap in hand; Dulcie touched it to the lips of her sex. Her breath left her in a rush and she shivered as the slick bar taunted the hard bud of her clit. Dulcie sighed and continued to touch herself.

* * *

Jack climbed the stairs and entered his guest room after washing his hair in the bathroom on the first floor. He heard a strange scraping in the hallway. He was undressing for bed but was still wearing his trousers. He cracked the door open and watched as maids carried water into Dulcie's room. They bid her good night and left her, closing the door behind them.

After waiting a few moments, Jack crept across the hall and quietly opened Dulcie's bedroom door. She rose from the water, her hair slick, water beading on her shoulders. Jack stopped breathing, terrified he'd reveal himself.

He watched as she washed herself, the heady scent of freesia filling the room. She gasped and Jack wondered if he made some sound but knew he hadn't when her head tipped back and she sighed in pleasure. His cock hurt with his need of her but he stayed and watched.

She reached out to the small table beside the tub, dropped a dripping cloth and picked up a bar of soap. Though he couldn't see what she was doing, he knew. The catch of her breath, the sigh that turned into a tortured moan told him what she was doing with that bar of soap.

Jack felt as though he was going up in flames. Dulcie whimpered his name as she reached back to grip the edge of the tub behind her head. Her cries grew louder and her head thrashed from side to side. Jack wanted to go to her, bring her to climax with his fingers, his mouth, his cock but he couldn't.

She didn't hate him, he knew, but she was hurt. Had he offered for her himself, long ago, rather than taking her parents' offer, things might be different. They could have been married for years now if he had asked her to marry him during her first season. Jack had been worried she was too young. When that bastard Bartel had asked her parents for their youngest child and they'd agreed, Jack had been devastated.

When he had heard about Dulcie and her family walking in on the orgy Bartel had been hosting in his London apartments, Jack had been unable to staunch the relief he'd felt. He had seen her the next day, held her as she'd cried. Her tears had ripped into his gut but he couldn't have been happier with the dissolution of her betrothal. He'd been even happier when she had confided in him that her tears were not for a love lost, but for the humiliation she and her family had suffered. Dulcie had called herself a fool. A fool to believe someone as seemingly perfect as Bartel had truly wanted her. Jack had taken her by the shoulders and looked into her eyes as he told her that she was perfect and any man who didn't know that and grovel at her feet was an imbecile.

He had been about to kiss her even though he had thought her too young. He was going to curl his arms about her and hold her close and take his first taste of her. Dulcie had moved first, though, wrapping her arms around his waist and burying her face in his shoulder. Jack had lost his nerve and merely hugged her back.

It hit him now how similar this situation was. He was holding back, staying away, giving her time to heal. Except this time was deliberate. She needed to get past her anger. He would be here when she did.

Jack focused his eyes on her. He watched as Dulcie lost control, listened as she keened his name on her completion. Jack stepped back, silently closing the door as he left. In his room, Jack undressed to his skin. A basin and jug of steaming water sat atop a dressing table along with soap, a cloth, and a thick towel.

He washed himself, thinking of Dulcie. He quickly cleansed all of his body but his shaft. Like his love, he dropped the cloth and used just the soap and his hand. Once he had a heavy layer of lather, Jack dropped the soap and washed his cock and balls thoroughly. He didn't miss a spot, went over them all again and again. Dulcie's voice whispered though his mind, asking to let her do it for him.

Jack tightly squeezed his eyes shut and pretended it was her washing his painful erection. It didn't take much time, minutes, maybe seconds before he grabbed up the soaked cloth and came on it. Jack's chest heaved for a few moments. He carefully rinsed his softening cock and hanging balls. He laughed, thinking that was likely the cleanest they'd ever been.

As he climbed into bed naked, he considered what they could do tomorrow. Something relatively harmless, but also with a certain level of intimacy. He thought a horse back ride would do nicely. He needed to mend the rift caused by his dishonesty. Oh, he had never lied to her about wanting her, about caring for her, but he hadn't been honest and told her about his arrangement with her parents. At the time, he had thought it best, believing she would think he didn't truly want her, as she thought now.

Jack had to make her understand he was taking the opportunity to catch the woman he wanted. Not that he was giving her parents, and ultimately her, the opportunity to snatch a very eligible man for her. He would make her understand that she was his and he was hers, any way he had to.

Chapter Ten

Dulcie came down stairs fidgeting with the riding habit the two maids had forced her into after she had awoken just after eight. She entered the dining room, frowning at the lack of breakfast waiting. Walking through to the kitchen, she found the servants eating their own morning meals. They stopped eating, stood, and looked at her expectantly.

"Did I miss breakfast?" Dulcie asked, feeling suspicious as she noted the number of eyes that pulled away from her gaze.

One of the maids curtsied to her and said, "Of course not, my lady."

The cook took Dulcie's hand in a motherly fashion and escorted her out of the kitchen. "It's such a beautiful morning; we thought you would perhaps like to eat outside."

The cook continued to guide Dulcie along as her dread continued to grow. "I think not. I would prefer to eat in the dining room, or perhaps the solar." She tried to dig in her heels but the cook was larger than Dulcie and very strong for a woman more than twice her age.

When the cook opened the front door, still without releasing Dulcie, she knew she was in trouble. Pulled out onto the fieldstone steps, Dulcie swallowed her anger as she looked at Jackson. He sat atop his large grey stallion with her little grey mare standing next to them. That wasn't a surprise considering the horse was a birthday present from Jackson a few years ago.

The buff-colored breeches faithfully skimmed Jackson's legs, showing every curve of muscle and bone. They buttoned just above the calf-length black leather riding boots. His navy blue cut-away riding jacket looked as tight as a corset, accentuating the breadth of his chest and shoulders. A cream and pale blue brocade vest peaked out from under the jacket, stretched taut over his lower belly. A cream cravat, tied simply, brought attention to his strong chin and jaw line.

Dulcie had to force herself to breathe deeply several times before she could speak. "What is going on?"

Jackson smiled and Dulcie felt her knees give a tiny bit. "I thought it would be nice to go for a ride before breakfast. I was hoping you would join me."

"No," Dulcie said without hesitation.

"Now, Lady Dulcie, you shouldn't be rude to guests. His lordship would just like the pleasure of your company." The cook patted her hand and smiled sweetly.

Dulcie didn't want the house staff to think poorly of her for being ungracious. Though Neil knew something was wrong between herself and Jackson, she didn't believe the footman knew what. Dulcie sighed, filling the sound with resignation. In her mind she plotted. She would make him pay for that little deceit and for convincing the members of the staff to help him.

*   *   *

She was thinking too hard. His Dulcie was trying to think of something deceitful. Jack could feel it. He could also see it in the crease between her delicate brows. Dulcie was fantastically bright but didn't have a cruel bone in her lush body. She had to work hard to come up with something that would intentionally hurt someone.

They had ridden for nearly an hour and now Jack was spreading a blanket near a creek. The gentle sound of flowing water, the chirping of the birds that had yet to migrate for the winter, the soft rustling of autumn-turned leaves made this small spot perfect for a picnic. From the package the cook put together Jack pulled out sweet buns, sliced fruits, slices of ham, and a flask filled with wine.

He looked up and watched Dulcie pace back and forth on the bank of the creek. One hand was curled into a fist against her hip as she chewed on the thumbnail of the other. She stopped, looked at him quickly then shook her head and resumed her pacing. Jack bit back a laugh but couldn't hold in a small smile. She was adorable.

"Dulcie, come and eat." His voice was slightly stern, trying to keep his merriment quiet.

She turned to him and squared her shoulders. "Perhaps I do not want to eat, Cornell. And don't think to order me about on my parents' land. I understand the three of you don't believe I can cope without interference, but I assure you, I am quite capable."

That annoyed Jack a bit. He had never thought of Dulcie as unable to do anything. He knew she was intelligent, had a wicked sense of humor, and was kind and gentle. He had seen her weather being the object of cruel remarks and crueler people. Only once had her humiliation been too great. He remembered the whispers even while her parents had hidden her for several seasons.

New scandals always arose but if something could be even distantly compared to a previous occurrence, it was. Members of the *ton* loved dwelling on the embarrassment and pain of others. If they could relive it, live vicariously through memories, they did. They also used it to distract others from their own demons. Whenever he had heard Dulcie whispered about, he made certain the person understood he was... displeased.

"Come and eat, Dulcie. Please." He held his breath as she turned away from him. Her arms were folded across her front, curving her back. She looked as though she was trying to fold in on herself, hide inside of herself. Jack wanted to go to her and wrap her in his arms. He would tell her he loved her if she would listen, but he knew she would not.

Curls danced across her nape as she shook her head. Her spine stiffened; her shoulders straightened. When she turned to face him a small, strained smile curved her lush lips. Jack was not certain if that boded ill or well.

Dulcie joined him on the blanket, curling her legs out to her side. He gave her half of the breakfast and watched her pick at it while he ate. She nibbled at a few items but left most of it uneaten. He would not have his Dulcie making herself sick.

Before she could defend herself, Jack toppled Dulcie to the blanket and covered her body with his. He straddled her hips, using his knees to pin her arms to her sides. Her breasts cushioned his chest. Dulcie tried to buck him off and Jack felt himself grow hard. She opened her mouth and Jack dropped a bite-sized piece of cinnamon cake between her teeth.

Dulcie growled but chewed and swallowed. When it looked like she would try to speak again, Jack dropped a large blueberry in her mouth. He didn't give her another opportunity to speak. He fed her little bits of food until most of her plate was clean. She would buck and try to roll when he would relax but Jack was always ready for her to try and escape.

For a moment he wondered if he was sick. Thinking of her tied to his bed, helpless under him as she was now, was testing his control. She tried again to free herself. Dulcie's breasts pressed against his chest and her hands groped around until they landed on his buttocks. Her hands tightened as she tried to drag him up and shift him off of her.

Jack couldn't stop himself. He pressed his groin into her soft belly and claimed her lips in a deep kiss. Dulcie shrieked into his mouth but he was relieved when she didn't bite down on his tongue. Jack curled one hand around her neck, his thumb caressing her jaw. His other hand worked between them to cup her breast.

Dulcie stiffened a moment before sighing and softening into his touch. Her entire body loosened and her tongue engaged his in the kiss. Rather than trying to push him out she invited him in and Jack nearly groaned at her welcome. He was able to stop himself by remembering the night before. She would have allowed him to touch her had he not spoken.

Dulcie moaned and tried to spread her legs. Jack shifted and raised Dulcie's skirts until he could lie between her thighs, pressing his cock against her pussy. A voice in the back of Jack's mind begged him to stop. He wasn't supposed to be seducing Dulcie. He was supposed to be talking to her, begging her to understand.

He tried to pull away but Dulcie wrapped her arms and legs around him. He couldn't contain his groan as she pumped her hips against him. The front of his trousers became damp as Dulcie grew wet. He had to stop, before it was too late.

Jack tore his lips from Dulcie's and buried his face against her neck. "Love, we must stop."

"No." Her breathing was labored and her hips pumped faster. "I am so close."

Jack swore. He would deprive himself anything, but not Dulcie. He ground his hips against hers and she soon began to shake. "Yes," she gasped, "more."

"Please, Dulcie, please come." He panted against her ear. His hips moved faster, gently rubbing and grinding his erection against her clitoris.

Dulcie cried out, her body convulsing. As her hold on him slackened, Jack pulled away, rolling to the blanket beside her. When he felt her hands groping at the buttons of his trousers he jumped up and put some distance between them.

"I did not mean for that to happen, Dulcie. I wanted to be alone with you so that we might have the chance to talk." Jack leaned his forehead against the trunk of the tree they picnicked under, trying to slow his heartbeat.

"There is nothing to talk about." Her voice was cool and distant.

Jack turned on her. "What do you mean there is nothing to talk about? What of us? Our future together? I made an error in judgment, yes, but please do not throw away everything because of that."

She rose first to her knees then to her feet, smoothing her skirts as she stood. "There is nothing to throw away. Honestly, Cornell, it hasn't even been a month that you have shown an interest in me. Prior to then you treated me as my brothers do; as a pleasant annoyance. Not that it matters. How do you think word of any betrothal would be received once your parents hear of what happened at Chelsey's ball?"

"They will be ecstatic," Jack exclaimed.

Dulcie's eyes bulged and she threw her hands into the air. "They will be mortified! In the eyes of the *ton* I am no better than a whore. A whore with lofty aspirations, I'll grant you, but one nonetheless."

"Don't you ever call yourself that word again! You are not a whore, Dulcie." Jack closed the distance between them and grabbed her by the upper arms. He shook her as he spoke. Pain lacerated him that she could think of herself in such a way.

"Men can act any way they wish to in our society, Jackson." Her voice was barely above a whisper. "Before and after marriage they can have mistresses. There are even those who prefer men in their bed and do not bother to hide the fact. They drink, gamble, engage in deviant sexual practices and yet when a woman slips, even a little, even once, she is condemned. Society will call a dishonorable man rambunctious and an unfortunate woman a whore. It is the way of our lives, Jackson."

Dulcie yanked her arms from his hands and ran for her horse. He allowed her to get into the saddle and ride away. It was obvious she needed time alone, as did he. She was correct about the way the *ton* worked. There were different rules for men and women. It was possibly even true that they were being vicious about her in London. Whispering about her and of their indiscretion at every available event. She was wrong about him, but Jack was beginning to fear it was too late to prove that to her.

Chapter Eleven

It had been two days since the picnic by the stream and Dulcie had seen neither hide nor hair of Jackson. He was still in the house, of that she was sure. She could hear him roaming the halls, smell him after he had been in a room, and feel him throughout the house. She wasn't sure whether to be happy he was still at Rothshire or curse him for not leaving.

If he left, she could discount all of his pretty words as lies. If he stayed... if he stayed, she had a feeling it meant even more than he was saying. She didn't understand why that should scare her so except that she was so confused and it seemed so hard to trust him now.

The library doors opened behind her and Dulcie held her breath.

"My lady?"

Dulcie sighed heavily but put as much cheer as she could into her voice. "Yes, Neil?"

"The Marquess is here," the interim butler announced.

"Yes Neil," Dulcie replied dryly, "I am aware of that."

"Forgive me, miss. I mean your brother and his wife. In fact both of your brothers as well as your sister, their spouses, and their children have just arrived."

Dulcie popped up from her seat and hurried to the door. "What?"

"Yes, miss. And I am sorry to tell you they have already seen the Marquess of Torningate." Dulcie could hear in his voice that he was not sorry to tell her that at all.

As she entered the hallway, Dulcie could hear shouting and cursing. Dulcie lifted her skirt above her slippered feet and ran to the group at the front door. A physical fight was close to breaking out; William had Jackson by the lapels.

Miles caught her before she could throw herself into the fray. "Stop it! Let him go!"

"He shouldn't be here, Dulcie. After all he's done...." William cut a quick look at her before turning back to Jackson and Daniel.

"He didn't do anything I did not allow him to do!"

Silence rang out after her exclamation. Her brother and brother-in-law released Jackson. He jerked his clothing back into place. Miles' arms tightened around her momentarily before releasing her and stepping away. Her sister and sisters-in-law and William's children stood in the doorway of the front drawing room.

"Dulcie—" William stepped toward her but she held up her hand between them.

"We will finish this later." She patted her hair and took a deep breath before plastering a smile on her face. Dulcie turned to her niece and nephew, going down on one knee to match their heights. "Hello, my loves!"

The three and four year olds ran into her arms and she hugged them tight. "Come along, goslings. Let's see what there is to play with in the nursery."

She stood and led them to the stairs. William's son Jacob tugged on her finger. "I'm not a goslin' anymore, Auntie. I'm a dragon." Jacob bared his tiny white teeth and curled his short pudgy fingers into claws.

"A dragon?" Dulcie gasped. "Oh no, Clarissa, what will we do?"

"We must run, Auntie," her niece cried, laughing at her younger brother's antics.

They went up the stairs. Dulcie took her time. The children's legs were too short to go very fast and in the end she carried them the rest of the way from the landing half way up the stairs. She spent her day laughing and playing with her niece and nephew.

Dulcie hadn't realized she had already begun imagining the children she and Jackson could have had together. The children she could have raised and loved and taught. Children she had never before believed would be possible because she never truly believed there was a man out there for her to love.

That night Dulcie begged off dinner claiming a headache. When her brothers and sister came to her door after the children were put to bed, she turned them away telling them they could speak on the subject tomorrow.

It was sometime after midnight when she went to the kitchen to heat water for a cup of tea. Jackson was already there. His black hair was soft. He wore only a pair of black trousers and a white shirt.

"Would you like a cup of tea, Dulcie?"

It didn't surprise her that he knew she was there. She always seemed to know when he was about as well. Tonight she was distracted but, truth be told, when she had seen the glimmer of light coming through the door, she had hoped it would be him. "Yes, thank you."

She took a seat at the servants' table and thanked him when he set the cup in front of her. He sat opposite her, not looking at her, simply sat there, staring into his cup. It was horrible that their years of friendship had been reduced to this – this awkward silence in the middle of the night.

"I never meant to hurt you, Dulcie," Jackson said softly.

Dulcie sighed. "I know," she conceded.

"May I ask why an arranged marriage is such an abhorrent idea?" Jackson still didn't look at her.

"Honestly? To spend the rest of your life with someone paid to take you? Whether or not they wanted you? I've been told my entire life how undesirable I am to men, Jackson. I... I just want what the rest of my family was so lucky to find. People to love them, not for titles or money, but for who they are, for their minds and their hearts."

"And you are so certain we could never have had that?" Jackson finally looked at her.

Dulcie took a large sip of her tea as she laid her heart out to be crushed. "You would have. I'm not so sure about myself."

He ran his hands through his hair. "Damn it, Dulcie, haven't I shown you—"

"What you've shown me is that you could have performed admirably well had you been stuck with me as your wife. But kisses and touching, Jackson, they are not the same as talking, as getting to know each other as we should have." Dulcie left the table and was almost out the door when he spoke again.

"I will be leaving tomorrow. I have some matters to set to rights with your family before I go and then I will be heading back to

London. Perhaps, someday, you will stop being angry. And perhaps I will still be waiting."

I hope so, Dulcie thought to herself.

*   *   *

Jack had asked Dulcie's siblings to meet him in their father's study after their morning meals. Daniel, Arian, and Reagan insisted they be allowed to attend any meeting that involved the welfare of *their* *pixie*. Everyone loved Dulcie and considered her theirs. If only she would allow him....

He shook the thought away as he looked at the six people across the room. The men looked at him with hard, angry glares. The women's gazes carried pity. He wondered if they understood. If they knew how much he cared and how much it was killing him to walk away. He sighed and leaned back against the bookshelves behind him.

"I know you don't want to believe this, Will, but your sister means everything to me. I never wanted to hurt her. I never wanted to disgrace her."

"Then why the hell didn't you just stay away from her?" William stepped forward threateningly but Jack made no
defensive gesture.

"I would imagine for the same reason you never stayed away from Arian," he replied, a sad smile on his face. "Tell me you never held her before the vows were said."

William charged up to him until the toes of their boots bumped and crumpled Jack's cravat in his fist. "Are you maligning my wife's character?"

"No, old friend, I am maligning yours. I remember our youth. We raised Hell a time or two. You did not go to your marriage bed pure as the driven snow, Will." Jack laughed into William's reddening face.

"I may not have, but Arian did," Dulcie's brother replied.

"Ahem, darling...." Arian's light voice called from across the room.

William turned his head to the side, his eyes stretching in her direction and a small smile curved his lips. "Ahh, yes," he said quietly.

He let go of Jack and took a step back. "It is not the same, however. Dulcie is my sister and the babe of the family. She has always had a hard time of it socially, and then there was her disastrous engagement to the heathen. This will be the final straw, I'm afraid. She had already told our parents she did not want to do another Season."

"Our Dulcie has so much to give," Reagan said. "I remember when I first met Miles. He tried so hard to get me to notice him but I never realized because no man ever wanted my attention. Dulcie became my dearest friend and introduced us and insisted I dance with him, all night if need be. That perhaps the other men in the room merely needed to see what I could do. It didn't matter. By the end of the evening I was in love with Miles and I thanked the saints for his little sister."

"When I first met Dulcie," Daniel chimed in, "she hit me with her parasol." The man chuckled. "She hadn't meant to. Another man was accosting Elaine and I was coming to her rescue. So was Dulcie. Just as she was bringing the umbrella down on the man's head, I stepped in to pull him off my love. Without missing a step she apologized to me and continued to beat the man. I stood there feeling completely useless until she suggested I help her sister into the nearest shop and send for a constable.

"Elaine had started yelling at me for leaving little Dulcie all alone with her attacker. Dulcie was still hitting the man and refused to stop until the constable arrived." Daniel looked at him and frowned. "You see, Cornell, we all love Dulcie and will protect her to the end. Even from a man we call a friend."

Jack chuckled sickly, shaking his head. "You never really understood, did you? Any of you?"

He pushed away from the bookshelves and walked to the door. He made his way up to his room where he spent the day packing what he'd brought with him. When he came to the box containing Dulcie's gifts, Jack couldn't bring himself to take them home. He would leave them at Rothshire.

Jack sat at the writing desk in the corner of the room and tried to compose a letter to Dulcie. He had never considered himself a poetic man and his lack of consideration was spot on. The words would not flow onto the paper as they should have. When Neil came up to inform him lunch and then supper was served, he declined the invitations, asking merely for tea then brandy.

He heard footsteps and muffled voices and realized the siblings were retiring for the night. Jack stared at the sheet of paper in front of him. In all of the hours he had been sitting there, he had written only six words. Those words wavered in front of him; the result of more than a little brandy.

Disgusted with himself, Jack rose from the desk and staggered to the bureau, hoping the cold water would clear his head. All he got for his trouble was being drunk, cold, and wet. He ripped off his cravat and shirt, using them to dry himself.

A light knock sounded at the door. "Jackson?"

Dulcie's voice was soft and hesitant. "Yes?" He asked just as softly, walking to the door. He rested his hand and his forehead against the wood, wishing he was holding her.

"I wanted to make certain you were not ill."

Jack bit back a bitter laugh. "Never fear, my sweet. I can leave tomorrow, just as I said I would."

She was silent for so long, Jack thought perhaps she had left. Just as he turned away from the door he heard her. "I did not say I wanted you to leave, Jackson. It merely hurts so much to have you stay."

Padded footsteps hurried away from his door, followed by a heavy thud. Jack's head throbbed almost as badly as his heart as he walked away from the door. How could everything have been mucked up so terribly? It was all going so well. He had been days away from officially asking Dulcie to marry him. He would have made the grand gesture of obtaining her parents' approval which he'd already had. Now he had nothing.

It was impossible to believe. This wasn't how events were supposed to happen. Since he could remember, Dulcie had been the girl he would marry. He had watched her grow up, waiting for the precise moment. Now she wanted nothing to do with him. His very presence in her house caused her pain. And the thought of losing her was causing his death. Perhaps that was surpassing melodramatic but it felt as though he was dying.

Jack stormed back to the bedroom door and opened it. He looked either way, looking for any of her brothers. When he saw that none stood guard, he crossed the hall and gently opened the door to Dulcie's room.

She sat at her dressing table. No maids were present; she must have sent them off directly after helping her with her clothing. Her copper hair was settled around her lawn covered shoulders. She drew the bristles of her silver brush through her hair, making the thick tresses gleam and fall in gentle waves.

Jack quietly closed the door behind him and moved so that he could see his own reflection in the mirror behind Dulcie. Her hand jerked to a stop. Dulcie laid the brush on her dressing table but did not turn to face him.

"What are you doing here, Jackson?"

Her soft voice tore at him, hardened his cock. He knew exactly why he had come to her room. "I've come to say goodbye."

Chapter Twelve

Dulcie stared at Jackson's reflection. He crept forward but it wasn't a timid motion. His was the movement of a predator. Jackson Cornell was stalking her. She rose from her perch on her vanity bench and slowly turned to face him. "Goodbye, Jackson. Safe journey. Now, if you wouldn't mind, I need to get to sleep."

"I do mind, Dulcie. I mind many things." Jackson walked toward her and Dulcie swallowed. His eyes were bright, his hair loose. She couldn't stop her eyes from taking in the skin left bared by his open shirt. Her fingers tingled as she imagined running them through the light dusting of dark hair covering his chest. Her temperature spiked as he stopped in front of her. The scent of man and brandy drifted over her, intoxicating her as much as if she had imbibed the alcohol herself.

"I mind that you believe I would ever intentionally hurt you. I mind that you are ejecting me from your life. I mind that you are more willing to let sadness and loneliness pervade our lives than allow us the love and happiness we could have together." Jackson wrapped his arms around her, pulling her hard against him. She could feel the erratic thump of his heart as it slammed against her own wildly beating one. "I mind that I will not again have the chance to hold you in my arms and kiss you, touch you like I should for the rest of our lives."

His mouth crashed down on hers, his tongue pressing inside to lash at hers. Jackson swept his hands down to her rear and cupped her hard, bringing her hips to him. He ground his pelvis into her belly, thrusting his hard cock against her softness. Heat tightened in her groin and had her growing wet between her thighs.

Jackson's mouth left hers to trail biting kisses down the side of her throat. "Jackson," she panted. "Please."

He growled against her skin making her shiver at the sensation. The world spun as he turned with her in his arms and walked her backwards to her bed. When her feet left the floor, Dulcie gasped. Jackson tossed her on the bed and stared down at her as he pulled his shirttails from his trousers and pulled the garment off over his head. His large hands moved to the buttons of his trousers and clumsily unfastened them.

He kicked the clothing away and stood naked beside the bed.

Jackson placed his hands on Dulcie's bare ankles and slid them slowly up her legs. His lips followed, moving up the calf of one leg, the thigh of the other. "Raise your hips, Dulcie." His voice scraped out of his throat, sounding harsh with the command.

"I...I can't. Jackson, please...." Dulcie was out of her head with desire. She knew she shouldn't allow him to touch her, tried to make herself tell him to stop but she couldn't.

"I will just have to find another way to my prize," he murmured softly. Dulcie's lungs squeezed when she felt Jackson's hot breath through the thin cloth of her night rail. His mouth and nose nuzzled the thatch of hair at the apex of her thighs. He opened his mouth over her cloth covered mound and closed his lips, tugging on the hair at her sex.

Dulcie moaned and pressed her hips up against his mouth. Jackson's tongue probed her through the cloth as his hands raised her nightgown. She cried out in dismay when his mouth left her and screamed in pleasure when he returned, this time without the cloth separating his mouth from her sensitive flesh. He slipped first one then two fingers inside of her. Jackson pressed his tongue between the lips of her sex and stroked from where his fingers penetrated her up her clit, which throbbed so hard her body jerked violently when he touched it.

His mouth and fingers left her sex and continued to push her gown up her body. Dulcie buried her fingers in Jackson's hair and tried to tug him back down. "Please, more."

"Believe me, love, you will get much more." He exposed her breasts and covered one nipple with his mouth.

Dulcie groaned as he sucked hard, pulling and distending her nipple almost to the point of pain. He turned to the other, rubbing his bristled chin against the stiff nub. Dulcie pressed his face to her breast and sighed when he finally opened his mouth and took the nipple inside. This one he suckled gently, using his tongue to roll it against the roof of his mouth.

Jackson pushed her arms over her head and removed her gown completely. His fingertips tickled the sensitive undersides of her arms. He pulled away from her breast, releasing her nipple with a loud, wet sound and brought his body up until he was aligned perfectly with her. His cock settled between her thighs, tight against her center. Jackson looked deep into her eyes. One of his hands coasted down her side and came between them. His fingers threaded through the hair at the apex of her thighs and then she felt the thick, round head of his cock pressing against her.

Jackson's eyes slipped shut as he slowly sank his body into hers. Dulcie bit her lower lip as her body stretched around his. His thumb rubbed gentle circles around her clit, making her hips jerk, making her take more of him in. She whimpered as he went deeper and deeper. He was large and it hurt.

He stopped and opened his eyes. "Hold on to me, love." With that, Jackson pulled back his hips and plunged in, breaking the barrier inside of her. Dulcie cried out at the burning pain.

Jackson kissed her, his tongue thrusting deep as he moved in and out of her body. He stopped petting her sex to pull her leg up and Dulcie wrapped both of them around his hips. The pain began to fade. Jackson continued to pump slowly in and out of her body. His thumb returned to torment her clit. She was grateful. Soon, pleasure began to bloom through her lower belly. It radiated outward, growing stronger and stronger. Dulcie worked her hips in tandem to Jackson's. She grabbed hold of his back, dragging her nails down to his rear and cupping and squeezing him hard.

"Please, please, yes, Jack. Don't stop." Sweat covered her body and his, making them slippery but that only added to the pleasure as his chest hair abraded her sensitive nipples.

"Never, I'll never stop..."

Dulcie missed the rest of what Jackson said as her world came apart. Her body spasmed over and over again. Jackson kissed her, muffling her screams of pleasure. He stopped moving and pulled away from her.

"Where are you going?" Dulcie gasped the question, wanting to feel Jackson lose control just as she had.

"Nowhere, love." Jackson rolled her to her left side and raised her right leg. He brought it across his chest and over his left shoulder. When he entered her this time he was deeper than before.

Still throbbing and sensitive from making love face to face, it didn't take long for Dulcie to come again. Nor did it when he turned her to her belly and put pillows under her hips. With her bottom in the air he thrust hard and fast. When she moaned at how good it felt he told her to be quiet.

She thought he must be jesting. She moaned again when he twisted his hips. Jackson's hand slapped her rear and Dulcie yelped, which earned her another smack. Surely she must be wicked for she enjoyed the sensation.

Dulcie reached between her legs and touched herself as Jackson had touched her. With every sound she made, he spanked her lightly, making her rear heat and her pulse pound. She came again and Jackson turned her to her back, returning to their original position.

He entered her and loved her so slowly and sweetly, tears came to Dulcie's eyes. He kissed her face, her neck, her shoulders. When she climaxed, Jackson came with her, his mouth on hers, his hands framing her face. He whispered to her how precious she was, how beautiful.

Dulcie fell asleep in his arms, hoping he would be there when she awoke. She knew, however, that her wish would not be answered.

Thirteen

Jack looked down at a sleeping Dulcie. His chest hurt at having to leave. Making love to Dulcie was everything he had ever thought it could be. The way she had responded to him; the feel of her around him.

He had to leave now. If he didn't, he would not have the strength to leave later. Hoping he wouldn't awaken her, Jack leaned down and lightly kissed her temple. "I love you," he whispered and left the room.

Stopping only to grab his boots and overcoat from his room, Jack made quick work of leaving the house. He hurried to the stables and saddled his horse. The sun was nowhere near rising but Jack didn't need the light. He knew the duke's land as well as he knew his own. He wouldn't make it to Torningate before he fell from his horse in exhaustion but that wasn't truly his intent. He needed to put distance between himself and Dulcie. He needed to forget, if only for a short time, that Dulcie even existed.

*   *   *

Sunlight and a cold bed greeted Dulcie as she woke. She turned to her back and looked at the canopy. "I will not be ashamed. I will not be ashamed of myself nor my actions."

Her whisper seemed to echo cruelly through her empty bedroom. Tears slipped from the corners of her eyes. "Damn it all," she whispered harshly as she scrubbed at the tears with her fists.

Dulcie threw back the covers and gasped as the cold morning air touched her naked skin. The blanket that usually lay across the foot of her bed was wedged between the corner of the mattress and its post. She wrestled it loose and wrapped herself as tightly as one might swaddle a baby. She left the bed and looked at the sheets. Just off center was a rust red stain. There were drops in other places as well.

Evidence of her final ruin stared her in the face. The tears had dried on her cheeks but she expected more. As she looked at the proof of her lost innocence, she expected to cry and rant and scream. She felt no inclination to do any of that.

She remembered last night. Every detail presented itself in full crisp color and definition. For all of his lies and all of his deceit, Jackson had given Dulcie one thing. And it was beautiful.

Dulcie dressed quickly, not bothering to ring for one of the few maids on hand. She even put the bed into some semblance of order, hoping they would see the smooth covers and not worry to change the linens. With a last look in the mirror to make certain her hair and dress were in place, Dulcie stepped into the hall.

Neil and the maids had the door to the guest room across the hall open. Several traveling bags and trunks were set outside the door. Jackson was nowhere in sight. Dulcie's stomach knotted. "Neil? Where is the marquess?"

Neil bowed to Dulcie and smiled gently at her. "It would appear that his lordship left sometime during the night. When the stable boy awoke this morning, he reported that he'd found the marquess' steed gone."

Dulcie's stomach dropped. He had run away in the dead of night. He hadn't waited to say goodbye. Bile burned the back of Dulcie's throat. Dulcie clutched her stomach. She walked down the stairs, her feet feeling like lead, and her heart threatening to beat from her chest.

As she entered the dining room Dulcie could hear the cacophony of a joyous breakfast. Her brothers, sisters and the children were talking and laughing as they ate. William saw her first.

"Pixie! Good Morning! Did you see that donkey left last night? A good thing, too. Miles, Daniel and I were going to throw him out if he didn't leave first thing this morning." William laughed and turned to their brother, toasting him in camaraderie.

She had promised herself she wouldn't cry. Not again. Not for Jackson. Then again, perhaps the tears rolling down her cheeks were not for Jackson.

"Dulcie? What's wrong?" Elaine left the table, followed closely by Reagan and Arian. When they reached her, a sob tore free of Dulcie's throat and she collapsed against her sister. "Dearling, please tell me what is wrong."

"Damn it, Dulcie!" William roared as he stormed toward the women. "Did he touch you?"

"William!" Arian admonished.

"Well?"

"Oh, do be quiet, Will! You stand there all high and mighty and holier than thou when you have absolutely no ground to stand upon. Name one day in your adult life you were pure and I will bow to you." Dulcie waited and watched as her oldest brother's face turned bright red. "I thought not."

She shoved past William and marched to the table, sitting on the side of the children as far from the other adults as possible. The rest of breakfast passed in an uncomfortable silence. Dulcie couldn't find her appetite. Her stomach was tied in so many knots she didn't know if she'd ever feel like eating again.

As the days went on, Dulcie avoided her brothers whenever possible, unable to tolerate their bruised eyes. She was hurt by their accusing stares. What time she didn't spend alone, which was most of her day, she spent in the company of her sisters and niece and nephew.

Dulcie rode out to the creek where she and Jackson had picnicked. She sat on the ground under the tree where he had brought her such physical joy. She no longer knew which was worse, being deceived by Jackson or being left by him.

Chapter Fourteen

Dulcie's parents returned to Rothshire. Though they normally would have stayed in London until all of the Christmas parties had come and gone, they had decided to return early since none of their children were in London for the holiday. Her mother talked of hosting her own Christmas soiree. Unfortunately, she wouldn't be able to invite many people as there were few not talking of Dulcie's indiscretion.

Immediately upon the duke and duchess's return, William took their father into the duke's study and closed the door. It wasn't long before Dulcie heard her name shouted throughout the manor house. *If nothing else,* Dulcie thought to herself, *it appears father is feeling better.*

Stiffening her spine, Dulcie walked into the study. Her father's face was bright red and her brother stood to the side of their father's desk. Dulcie was tired of William's domineering of late. Never had her brother treated her as he had in the past month. She wavered between crying over the change in their relationship and wanting to beat him about the head with a blunt object for treating her so cruelly when she needed his love and support.

"Sit!" Her father had his fists planted in the center of the desk and he kept his eyes off of her. "Please tell me what Will has told me is not the truth."

"It would all depend on what it is he has told you." Dulcie looked at her brother. She held his gaze until he cleared his throat and looked away. Dulcie began thinking of objects in the room she could use on her dear brother.

"He told me you and Cornell…. That you two…. Ah, damn it all." He rubbed a hand over his face and fell heavily into his large high backed chair. "You know what he told me, Dulcie. Why? How could you?"

Dulcie laughed bitterly. "Isn't it what you wanted father? For him to beguile me?"

"Your mother and I wanted to see you married, we wanted to see you happy. What if there is a child?" He looked her over a concerned frown creasing his forehead.

"I can tell you with all confidence that there is no child, father." When her monthly flow had come two weeks after making love to Jackson, Dulcie had cried. Even now she could
not say for certain if it had been in relief or disappointment.

"No, I suppose there is not. What has happened to you, Dulcie? Your cheeks have thinned and your figure is not as full as it once was," her father remarked.

Dulcie had found her appetite had waned since Jackson's departure. She no longer found pleasure in the things she once had such as music, reading, and food. "Nothing has happened, father."

The old man sighed. "Dulcie, you can go. Ask your mother to come in here. We have matters to discuss."

"Only if Will leaves with me." Her father and brother both began to protest. Dulcie held up her hand. "No, William is the oldest, next in line, a marquess with profitable lands of his own; all of this I know. He has also turned into a terrible busybody, as much of a gossip as many of the matrons of the *ton* and I will *not* have him, of all people, aiding to decide my future."

"Fine. Will, you won't be included in the conversation. Leave with Dulcie." Their father nodded toward the door.

"Father, it is my duty to Dulcie to help her protect her future." William huffed indignantly.

Dulcie was beginning to grow tired of how childish her brother was acting. Never had she known him to act like such an obnoxious adolescent, angry for not getting his way at every turn. Dulcie sincerely hoped the day would come that they could put this behind them and be the brother and sister they used to be. As for now, however, she would treat him as she treated his children when they were unruly. She would ignore him and allow his parents to settle the matter. Unfortunately for William, it took much more for the children to upset her than it was taking for him to.

"I will not leave unless he does." Dulcie stood her ground. She couldn't fathom where the Dulcie who was so docile for her family had gone. She did know, however, that she would no longer be cowed by heavy-handed men like her brother. Like Jackson.

"Go, Will," their father intoned.

William turned and scowled at Dulcie. She waited, making him precede her out of the room. Their mother stood outside the door and Dulcie stood aside, motioning her in and closing the door behind the smaller woman. Just to make certain William didn't misunderstand, Dulcie stood guard, her cheeks heating as she heard first her mothers outraged cry then her pained sobs.

The door flew open behind her, her father shouting her name. "Dulcie! Oh, Dulcie, sorry dear. Come in here. Your mother and I need to speak to you."

Dulcie once again entered her father's study.   Her mother sat in the large leather chair behind the desk, her face in her hands, her slim shoulders hunched. Dulcie felt her heart twist.

"Take a seat," her father said.

Dulcie sat in one of the wingback chairs before the fireplace. The heat of the fire barely warmed her as she sat and waited to hear her parents' decision. She rubbed her frozen hands together, trying to chafe some heat into her skin.

"We have decided to have a Christmas ball, Dulcie, here at Rothshire. We will invite all of the eligible titled gentlemen in England and your mother and I will choose a suitable match for you." Her father's voice was gruff, telling her he did not want to have to force her hand but that she had left him no choice. "The next day we will negotiate a marriage contract. We will have to provide a larger dowry to compensate for your indiscretion but I do believe we should be able to settle you with an agreeable husband."

Dulcie bit her lips to prevent herself from crying out. She didn't want an *agreeable husband*. She feared, however, that it might already be too late for what, or rather whom, she did want.

Chapter Fifteen

Christmas Eve had dawned that morning dull, damp, and cold. Had she been superstitious Dulcie might have believed the weather was an omen. As it were, she had little faith this night would bring more than humiliation for either her or her parents.

Dulcie sat at her vanity as two maids curled and coifed her hair. A deep burgundy velvet dress was laid across her bed. The center line of the bodice and skirt were golden satin. Stitching in the bodice made a diamond quilt pattern, garnet beads sewn in where the lines crossed.

Tonight her parents were going to choose a husband for her, or attempt to at any rate. Dulcie wasn't all together convinced it mattered how much curl they put in her hair, how much color they put on her cheeks, or how prettily they dressed her. What mattered was a man's willingness to look past her overly soft body, which none ever had. What mattered was a man's willingness to look past the spectacle she had made of herself at Lord Chelsey's ball, a highlight few would ever let her forget. What mattered would be a man's willingness to forgive her lack of purity, which was a farfetched notion, indeed.

Dulcie flinched as the maids pushed pins, tipped with jewel encrusted ladybugs, into her hair. Torn from her musings, Dulcie sighed frowning as they began to apply spots of color to her eyes, cheeks, and lips. She raised a hand to bat her offenders away and wash off the irritating cream. "Not to worry, milady, not much is needed with your lovely coloring," one maid commented. She rapped Dulcie's knuckles with the thin silver handle of the brush she was using to apply color to Dulcie's lips.

Once they were finished torturing Dulcie, they forced her into a corset and gown. She sniffed indignantly, pulling at the beautiful dress as though it were a sack. "I do not even see why I must attend. My parents are going to make the decision completely on their own. They have no need for me. I should be allowed to remain here in my room and not uncomfortably stuffed into this dress."

"Now, milady," said the same maid who had admonished her earlier. "If you want to know uncomfortable, I can tell you stories of the dresses and corsets that used to be in fashion. But that is not the true matter, love. Your parents are trying to do right by you and you have turned into a spoiled, petulant, rotten little child."

Dulcie could feel her cheeks heating under their paint. She turned her eyes down to the floor and folded her hands in front of her. If a member of the staff was willing to speak so plainly to her of her obnoxious behavior of late, she must truly be acting horribly.

"Now, I know your heart was broke, lass, but your parents are doing what they feel is best for you. So you will go downstairs tonight, dance with all of the gentlemen your parents direct you to, and acquiesce to your parents' decision. Do you understand, milady?"

"Yes," Dulcie said softly.

The maids helped her put on her burgundy slippers and touched up her hair. Miles came to escort her downstairs. Oliver announced her arrival. At the large double doors of the grand ballroom. Dulcie tightened her hold on her brother's arm, terrified she would drop from fright. Miles patted her hand and whispered, "It will be all right, love."

She knew he was lying. It would never be all right. Dulcie smiled brightly, her eyes tripping over all of the curious faces. Few of them looked at her with an ounce of the kindness they once did. Her smile didn't falter even as she tried to swallow her lump of fear.

At the foot of the stairs, Caressa came fluttering to her, wrapping her arms around Dulcie's waist. In Dulcie's ear she whispered, "I don't care what they say. You are my truest of friends."

Tears formed in Dulcie's eyes but she blinked them back as she returned Caressa's hug. "As you are mine."

They separated and Caressa followed as Miles escorted Dulcie to where their parents were stationed on a raised dais at the side of the room. She kissed each parents' cheeks and waited. With the exception of Arian, who was sitting with her two month old in the nursery, all of the brothers and sisters were present and she kissed them as well.

First to approach her was Frederick Gander. As the third son of the lord of Hillford he would be expected to either make his fortune on his own or marry into it. Apparently he had chosen the latter. By her brothers' disapproving scowls, she knew they didn't like him. Dulcie did not feel one way or the other about the man. When they had had the chance to meet, Frederick had always been cordial. He seemed even-tempered, was well-educated, and she had never heard tell of scandal in connection with his name. While he wasn't unattractive, she considered as they danced, he was rather unnoticeable. His hair was so fair it was practically the same shade as his very pale skin. His eyes were a medium shade of brown. His features were round and soft.

She was so intent on her study she hadn't realized he was speaking. "Your parents have a lovely home. Al-almost as l-lovely as their daughter."

She could tell by his stutter and sickly smile that he did not truly find her lovely. Dulcie smiled, understanding his discomfiture. Frederick frowned and a blotchy blush stained his cheeks. "Thank you."

The song ended and Frederick escorted her back to her parents. That was how the night progressed. Dulcie was passed from one unmarried gentleman to the next. It was a relief when Kirkland Perry came forward for his dance. Kirkland may be no more inclined to marry her than any other man in the room but she liked him well enough to consider him something of a friend.

He bowed over her hand, his lips grazing her knuckles. It struck Dulcie that Kirkland had never before done that. She wondered for a moment if he believed she would allow him liberties because of her past with Jackson. When he raised his head to look at her, however, she could see no sign of deception in his gaze.

Kirkland led her onto the parquet. A waltz began and more than a few dance partners left the floor. Dulcie mentally sighed. While he was a wonderful dancer, she did not fit Kirkland that way she fit Jackson.

She slammed her eyes shut and forced the thought away. She had to stop thinking of Jackson. It had been months since that night. *When would it stop hurting?*

"Dulcie? Are you all right?" Kirkland's voice broke through her memories. She opened her eyes and felt a tear she could not stop slip down her cheek. The song had not yet ended but Kirkland pulled her to the side. "Oh Dulcie." He wiped the tear away. "Come, you need some fresh air."

Kirkland led her out of the main doors of the ballroom. They somehow avoided her family and Oliver as well as the rest of the household staff, who were all busy with the party. They made their way to the front door where her escort hastily grabbed a coat and a thick shawl and stepped just outside.

Not caring who the fur-trimmed wool shawl belonged to Dulcie happily wrapped herself in its warmth. "Thank you," she murmured.

"Why are you doing this, Dulcie?" Kirkland asked.

"Pardon?"

"Why are you doing this to yourself and Jack? The two of you belong together. You would be happy together." Kirkland said quietly.

Dulcie chuckled bitterly as she stepped gingerly down the front steps. "Did the other men in there put you up to this? 'Go ahead, Kirkland, she likes you the best. Convince the cow she doesn't want to marry one of us.' Thank you very much."

"No, Dulcie, that isn't what this is about at all." Kirkland followed her, taking her shoulders in his hands and turning her to face him. "Let me tell you a story. It is about my years at Eton, then at Cambridge. Do you know who was one of my closest friends during those years? Jackson Cornell. Jack was brilliant at many things – mathematics, science, history – but what I liked most about him was his ability to tell a tale. And there was one character he told tales of most frequently. The strange thing was I knew this person. She was tall for a girl, had long red hair, brown eyes, and was the sweetest girl I knew. And Jack's favorite story to tell of her was how he was going to marry her one day.

"There was a problem though. I wanted her for myself, as did several other chaps we knew. When we went to university there would be nights several of the boys and I would go to one of our fathers' clubs and meet women of... questionable virtue. The few times Jack accompanied us he always found a woman reminiscent of the woman from his tales."

Kirkland released her shoulders and stepped away from her, turning away from her for a moment as if adrift in memories before returning to her. "One night I remember we had all been drinking, Jack and I much less than the others, to the point that the others passed out cold long before midnight. I told him that I would have you, Dulcie. That he could find someone else for the youngest Brighton child would be my bride. Do you know what he said to me?"

Dulcie shook her head. Kirkland walked up to her, coming close so that only a hairsbreadth separated them. "He said, 'I love her, Kirk. I think I must have loved her before I was even born for I don't remember a time I didn't love her. She is everything good in this world, everything good in me.' That gave me pause but something inside me still told me to reach for you." He lifted a hand to her cheek, grazing her cheek with his fingertips.

"Then, that summer at his parents' estate, I saw how you acted around him. How you blushed whenever he paid attention to you, how you laughed and smiled at him. How you would glance at him when he wasn't looking and look for him when he wasn't near. That was when I knew I had to look elsewhere for my bride. I could see that you were in love with him, too."

Dulcie shook her head. "How could you know when I didn't?"

"All I had to do was look at you looking at him. You were still young, Dulcie. You still had to grow and learn." Kirkland wrapped his free arm around her waist and caressed her jaw with his fingers. "Now, though, could you find room in your heart to love another?"

Kirkland lowered his lips to Dulcie's. His kiss was soft and gentle, his tongue gliding across her lips, entreating her to open. When she did, he explored softly. It was a beautiful kiss, one that would live in Dulcie's memories, she knew. But it did not touch her heart in the way Kirkland claimed he hoped it would.

He pulled back and looked into her eyes. "You do not feel as I do, do you Dulcie?"

"No, I am sorry, Kirkland." She wrapped her arms around him and hugged him close, laying her head on his shoulder. "I never knew you felt this way. You were always kind to me, certainly, but you never showed an interest in me. You always follow around after... smaller women."

Kirkland squeezed Dulcie close as if reluctant to let her go. "That was because I knew you and Jack were made for one another. To come between you two would have been wrong. I warned off the others who had their eyes on you. The only one to not listen was Bartel and that was because he was an ass who wanted to cause mayhem more than anything else."

"As for the women, it isn't just a body that suits me. And there is nothing wrong with yours, Dulcie, believe me. You are beautiful. I always thought so." Kirkland kissed the top of her head.

Dulcie uttered a choked, "thank you."

"Come along, love. We need to get you into the house before you catch your death." Kirkland escorted her back inside and took the shawl from her shoulders. "Before we go back into the ballroom, let me say one last thing. A lifetime is a long time to spend with someone you do not love and who does not love you. My parents, for the good face they show to the *ton*, have not had a happy marriage. They were both in love with other people when their parents forced them to marry one another. I'll admit, they are... friends but they have never truly loved each other."

Kirkland took her back into the ballroom and to her parents. He bowed over her hand, lingering over her knuckles and giving her a sad smile before walking away. Once he was out of earshot her mother said, "Where have you been? You missed your dance with the son of the Earl of Cardiff."

"I'm sorry, Mother. I wasn't feeling well. Kirkland took me outside, thinking it might help." Dulcie felt her cheeks heat thinking of the kiss Kirkland had given her.

A man with graying hair and mustache was making his way up the few stairs of the dais. "Here comes the Duke of Coddington. Try not to wonder off with him, please."

"Mother," Dulcie admonished quietly.

"Dulcie," Lady Moira returned. She sighed, "Dear, you only have a few more dances then you can retire for the night."

Dulcie nodded and accepted the duke's hand when he approached. For the next two hours Dulcie continued to dance. When her parents allowed her, she left the party and slowly climbed the stairs. At the top Dulcie stopped, pulled not to her door but to the door of the room Jackson had used during his stay.

Picking up a decorative oil lamp from a table against the wall, Dulcie opened the door and stepped inside. Maids had been in the room dozens of times since Jackson had left. As far as she could tell, no trace of him remained, but she felt closer to him nonetheless.

Dulcie walked around the room, letting her fingers touch on the fabrics covering the bed, the wood of the furniture. When she came to the desk, she found something odd. A small chest sat atop the desk, two crests were engraved on the front. One was her family crest, the other was Jackson's. On the top of the box, her fingers followed the letters DNB. The key was in the lock.

Dulcie lifted the lid and peered inside. Inside were a number of smaller wooden boxes. She picked up a small but beautifully painted square box from the center. Dulcie gasped when she opened it and found a beautiful diamond ring. Each box contained a beautiful piece of jewelry or a small trinket. One box held a gold locket; inside one half was a snippet of black hair, in the other were engraved the words *my heart is yours*.

Dulcie's chest ached with too much emotion. She laid the necklace on the desk, straightening the chain, trying to make sense of everything. Something caught her attention. The corner of a piece of paper peeked out from under the chest. Dulcie pulled it out and read the words scrawled in Jackson's elegant handwriting.

I love you. Please forgive me.

Sobs tore free from Dulcie's throat.

Chapter Sixteen

Jack looked out over the snow covered hills of the Torningate estate. His parents had tried to insist he join them a few miles away at their manor house in Waterton but he had promised to join them for dinner. For most of the day, Jack wanted peace, he wanted solitude, he wanted.... He wanted Dulcie.

"Ha!" Jack laughed bitterly at himself. He had a better chance of Father Christmas appearing before him.

"My lord, you have a visitor," Jack's butler, Wilcox, called from the door of his study.

Jack looked at the man over his shoulder. "I am not receiving any visitors today, Wilcox."

"And I am not leaving until you speak to me."

Very slowly Jack turned to see Dulcie standing just behind his butler. "Leave us."

"Yes, my lord." Wilcox bowed and left the room, closing the doors behind him.

Neither of them said anything for several minutes. He looked at her. Her eyes were red. She had lost weight since the last time he had seen her, hollowing her cheeks slightly and defining her collarbone. The glint of a gold chain caught his eye. She was wearing the locket.

She had found the box. He wondered when. He wondered if she had found anything else. Dulcie stepped forward and her scent of freesia and woman drifted toward him.

Dulcie was the first to break the silence. "How are you, Jackson?"

Jack didn't know what to say. He was half tempted to lie, to tell her he was wonderful. He couldn't. "I'm miserable, Dulcie."

She took another step toward him and Jackson took a step toward her. "So am I, Jackson." She looked away and chewed on her lip.

Jack took three large steps, almost closing the distance between them. "Why did you come, Dulcie?"

* * *

Jackson's whispered question steeled Dulcie's resolve. She looked into his eyes. "I came for you," she responded and closed the distance between them.

"Why?" Jackson placed his hands on her waist. Her knees went watery at his touch.

"Because I need you, Jackson. I need you by my side, day and night. I need to hold you in my arms and I need you to hold me. Because I love you, Jackson. More than anything."

Jackson kissed her, his mouth seizing hers. He kissed as if he were starving for the taste of her. Dulcie understood this for she felt the same way. Her hands roamed his body, threaded through his hair, tore at his clothing. She needed to feel his skin against hers. Jackson pulled away, took her hands in his and held them to his chest, and looked into her eyes. "I love you, Dulcie. I always have and I will for the rest of my days." He kissed her finger tips. "Say you will marry me."

"I will," she replied."

Jackson smiled and pulled her back into his arms, his hands going to the fastenings at the back of her dress. He stopped as the dress began to sag. "Come with me," he whispered, placing a kiss on the tip of her nose.

Jackson led her upstairs to his bedroom. He stood her before a full length mirror in the corner in the room and continued to remove her dress, kissing her skin as he bared her. He removed her half corset and shift and simply stared at her reflection as she stood nude before him.

"You are so beautiful, Dulcie. My love." His hands touched on her hips and slid forward to her stomach. He brought them up to cup her breasts, pulling and plucking her nipples to hard points. Dulcie dropped her head back to his shoulder, seeking his lips with hers.

Against her mouth he whispered, "You have lost weight, my love. We have to work on building your appetite."

Dulcie smiled. "Please do."

One of Jackson's hands slid down her body. He pressed his fingers between her legs, seeking her clit. Dulcie gasped and cried out as he massaged her. He pressed the nub harder and harder, faster and faster until she exploded. Dulcie cried out, "Jack!"

Jackson held her until her shudders became shivers then took her hand and led her to his bed. He pulled back the blankets and guided her to lay back. Dulcie turned onto her side, watching her love as he undressed for her.

Once he was naked, Dulcie sighed at the sight of his beautiful body. The long, lean muscles of his arms and legs, the chiseled curves of his chest and stomach made her salivate. The sight of his long, hard cock made her shivers begin anew.

Jackson climbed in next to her into the bed. His hands smoothed over her body, tracing her curves, kissing her everywhere. When his teeth tugged her nipples, Dulcie arched her back, begging for more. He suckled and licked them, making her moan. Jackson kissed a line down the center of her body. Her hips bucked when she felt his hot breath ruffle the hair covering her sex.

"Please, no, I cannot wait this time." Dulcie pulled on Jackson's hair. He rose above her, positioning the head of his cock at her entrance.

"I love you, Dulcie." Jackson thrust inside of her, deep and hard.

Dulcie felt contractions begin deep in her womb. "I love you, Jackson," she replied.

He smiled down at her and began to move, slow and deep. It felt so glorious, Dulcie never wanted it to end. Already the contractions grew stronger, however. Dulcie wrapped her legs around Jackson waist and pumped her hips against his. The feel of his cock moving inside of her was heaven and hell, salvation and sin.

Jackson moved faster, his hips pumped harder. "More, please. Don't stop," she begged.

"I'll never stop. I'll never stop loving you," Jackson gasped.

Dulcie cried out as she came, her vision graying. She grabbed Jackson's back, burying her nails into his skin as her climax went on and on.

Jackson shouted her name as he ground his hips against her. Dulcie held him against her. She could feel her tears streaming from her eyes. Her lover lifted his head and kissed her tears from her face. "Did I hurt you, Dulcie?

"No, that was beautiful, Jackson. Simply beautiful."

Jackson smile as he looked down into her eyes. "We will be married as soon as possible, even if I have to buy a special license. You are not getting away again, Dulcie Nan Brighton."

Dulcie laughed. This year for Christmas she received everything she could ever want. A man to love that loved her in return, a genuine proposal of marriage, and all of it with Jackson Cornell. Her hero, her love, her heart.

Epilogue

Eight Months Later

Dulcie held out her arms and took very small steps backwards. "Come along," she said sweetly to the smiling, nearly toothless toddler. "Come along, Haley. Come to Auntie Dulcie." The sunlight glinted off the sparse blond curls of Miles and Arian's daughter.

The little girl giggled and her chubby arms reached for Dulcie as she followed along until Dulcie finally let the baby catch her. She swung the little one high in the air and around in a circle and the child laughed even harder. Dulcie laughed with her and brought her niece close to her for a hug. She looked up to see her husband speaking to her brother Miles. He looked at her and even at this distance she could see the softness that overtook his features.

She carried Haley to Arian and the little girl gurgled happily at the sight of her mother. Dulcie sat next to her sister-in-law who commented, "That man has a brooding look about him."

Dulcie looked at Jackson and smiled. "He says that he enjoys having our time together but every time he sees me with one of the children his face softens in such a way that I wonder if he truly means it."

Elaine laughed. "I don't doubt he means it, dear. However, a man can't help but picture the woman he loves caring for a child that is a part of them both."

Reagan clicked her tongue before saying, "Not that they give you any peace when you are carrying the child. Constantly moving things out of your way as though you're some great beast without the ability to move around objects."

The others laughed and Reagan huffed, which only made them laugh harder. Finally Reagan joined in. Four shadows fell over their sunny spot and the women looked up to smile at their beloved husbands. Jackson held his hand out for Dulcie and she took it and rose. "Is it time to leave already?"

"Only if we hope to reach Torningate tonight, my love." Jackson looked deeply, hungrily into her eyes and Dulcie knew she wanted to return to their manor house tonight.

She turned to her brothers and sister and their spouses and waved the playing children in so that she could kiss them all goodbye. The children complained that they had only just arrived a few days before but Dulcie promised that they would visit again soon.

Her sister and sisters-in-law smiled knowingly at her as they hugged her. Conversely, her brothers and brother-in-law frowned as they hugged her. Her husband smiled as he shook their hands. As they walked away Dulcie whispered to Jackson, "It isn't nice to tease them. They may still decide a night in the village gaol is worth thrashing you."

He kissed her nose. "If it would make them feel better I might just let them do it. But then I couldn't do this."

"What?" She asked, then quickly wished she hadn't when he lifted her high and wedged her into the carriage. Dulcie looked at her husband through the small door as he jumped up through it and laughed at his antics as she batted his hands away.

"Take me and my lady home, Lon."

"Yes, my Lord."

Jackson worked his hands up Dulcie's legs and she laughed as she pretended to fight off his advances. He spread her thighs and pulled her bare groin tight to his restrained one. "So tell me, Marchioness," he said silkily, "what can I give her to make my lady-wife happy for her birthday? Aside from the beautiful gala I have planned for her two weeks from tonight."

"Your heart," Dulcie demanded.

"I gave it to you long ago," Jackson replied.

"Your soul," she said softly this time.

"The good Lord made our souls as one so that we may go through Eternity together forever. You have had that even before you were born," he returned just as softly.

"Your love," Dulcie whispered.

"Forever," Jackson promised.

Dulcie remained quiet for a moment. When she spoke again her voice was choked. "Your child."

Jackson smiled. "Your will." He kissed her lips softly and set about to fulfilling her wish.

Courting Caressa

Prologue

Caressa Davenport stared out of one of the tall, thin windows that flanked the front doors. Never had she imagined she would feel jealousy toward her best friend. Then again, never had she thought to see Dulcie in Kirkland Perry's arms, his lips pressed to hers.

When Caressa had watched them leave the ballroom, she had been worried something was wrong with Dulcie and had followed as soon as the dance was through. She had reached the front hallway just in time to see them step out the door. They had been talking and Kirkland had appeared agitated, then he had pulled Dulcie close and kissed her. The moonlight glinted silver on Kirkland's dark brown hair as he brought his head down to Dulcie's titian one.

Now, the pair stood locked in each other's arms. Steam puffed from lips as they spoke. Caressa watched for as long as she could. Her heart was thumping painfully in her chest. After all of these years waiting for Kirkland to offer for her, she had her answer as to why he never had.

Caressa returned to the ballroom, finding an empty seat in a darkened corner. It wasn't long before she could see flashes of Dulcie on the parquet. People whispered how lovely she was beginning to look as she lost weight.

Though she had been torn apart by what she had spied, Caressa wanted to stamp on the feet of those who would suggest Dulcie was ever anything but beautiful. Her head spun with love and jealousy. Her head began to throb. Caressa closed her eyes and breathed deeply, in through her nose and out through her mouth, and rubbed her temples in an attempt to relieve the pressure.

"May I have... Lady Davenport? Are you all right?"

The air seized in Caressa's chest. Kirkland's deep, slightly gruff voice was soft and filled with concern. She opened her eyes to find her gaze filled by Kirkland's handsome face. He had sat down in the chair next to hers and was leaning across her so that he could look into her face.

It was too dark to see the brilliant green of his eyes but she felt them staring into hers. He picked up her hand and rubbed it between his. "Caressa?"

She swallowed hard past the lump in her throat. Caressa wished she hadn't seen them, silvered by the moonlight, but wishing wouldn't make it so. "I am fine, Mr. Perry. My head ached a bit was all." She smiled as brightly as she could, hoping it would convince him nothing was wrong.

Kirkland returned her smile. "Then may I have this dance?"

Caressa held her breath and nodded. She rose from her seat and allowed Kirkland to lead her to the dance floor. If she couldn't have his heart, at least she could have this dance.

Chapter One

Caressa and her parents, The Duke and Duchess of Davenport, sat in the chapel pew, watching her friend, Dulcie Brighton marry Jackson Cornell. At the end of the ceremony she would be the new Marchioness of Torningate. Dulcie looked beautiful. Her dress was layers and layers of fine white cotton. Small pink ribbon roses dotted the long skirt and silver lace trimmed only the empire waistline. Her thick red hair was twisted into curls that cascaded like a waterfall from a braided knot atop her head. Jackson looked exceptionally handsome dressed in a royal blue coat and fawn trousers. His gold tasseled Hessians gleamed in the morning light streaming through the chapel windows. His black hair was caught at his nape with a black cord, sweeping his hair from his face, showing his striking features.

She was happy for her friend, truly. Knowing everything Dulcie had felt – never believing she was good enough for Jackson, her disbelief that someone as handsome as Jackson would want a full-figured lady – Caressa couldn't be happier for her dearest friend. She remembered how elated Dulcie had been when Jackson had declared his intentions and begun to court Dulcie. She also remembered her friend's heartbreak and insecurity when she had learned her parents had asked Jackson to marry her. Caressa was delighted that Dulcie decided to follow her heart and had forgiven Jackson. Wickedly, she was delighted for more than one reason. It was that reason that was coloring her excitement of the day.

Dulcie's sister by marriage, Reagan, and her eldest niece attended her. When Dulcie had asked Caressa, she hadn't been able to bring herself to accept. She was still torn between her sisterly love for Dulcie and her jealousy that her friend had been kissed by Kirkland Perry. *Kirkland....*

Caressa's eyes wandered to the opposite side of the chapel. Kirkland sat with his own family. His curling brown hair was the color of her favorite chocolate treats, cut ruthlessly short to discourage the curls from growing out of control as they did when he was a child. His firm, defined lips were set in a hard line as he watched the ceremony. Three lines were formed between his emerald green eyes, giving away the frown he was obviously trying to hide. He looked away as Dulcie recited her vows. Caressa bit the inside of her cheek at the dull, painful thudding of her heart.

She had waited so long, gently declining when any other man had asked for her hand. Waiting for Kirkland to offer for her. Now she knew why he never had.

The ceremony ended and, amidst the cheering people of Rothshire, Dulcie and her new husband left the chapel. The townspeople offered happy wishes to the smiling couple. Everyone followed the newly wedded pair back to the Duke of Rothshire's estate where a large breakfast buffet awaited.

The house was buzzing with activity. Oliver had every available hand and some Caressa assumed to be hired on for the day, as she didn't recall ever seeing them before, taking coats and hats, carrying about trays of food and beverage. When Tory, the stable boy, slid across the hallway floor, dressed in fine livery two sizes too big, Caressa released a startled laugh. Yes, Oliver had every available hand helping with the reception.

Entering the large dining room, Caressa took a deep breath, squared her shoulders and walked up to Dulcie and Jackson. A forced smile curled her lips as she hugged her friends. "I am so very happy for the both of you!" Her voice seemed to screech falsely inside of her own head.

"As am I," a deep, soft voice said from behind her.

Caressa looked over her shoulder at Kirkland. She had been so certain he hadn't been in the room when she had decided to approach Dulcie. Kirkland leaned forward and kissed Dulcie's cheek. Caressa felt her chest burn but smiled and hugged Dulcie again.

She watched Kirkland shake Jackson's hand. Kirkland congratulated Jackson on marrying "one of the most wonderful women in all of the English Empire."

Jackson laughed. "I am merely lucky I was finally able to convince her *to* marry me."

The men continued to talk and laugh. When Dulcie rubbed her back and tweaked her earlobe, Caressa realized she was still holding on to Dulcie as if for dear life. Dulcie looked into her eyes. "What is wrong?"

"Nothing." Caressa cursed her voice as it broke on the single word. She felt tears well in her eyes.

Dulcie walked with her to the other side of the room. "Please, Caressa, tell me what is the matter."

Caressa bit her tongue before she could, indeed, tell her friend everything that was upsetting her. She forced another smile and even a small laugh. "I must admit to just the tiniest spot of jealousy. Please forgive me, Dulcie. I am so very happy for you and Jackson."

Dulcie smiled that sweet, beautiful smile of hers. "There is nothing to forgive. You could have any man in England. I am willing to wager I will be watching you take your own marriage vows before the year's end."

Caressa knew she could not have any man she wanted, the one man she wanted. "I certainly hope you do not wager very much," Caressa said darkly.

Dulcie looked at her as though she had grown a horn. Caressa forced another laugh. "Come, I should return you to Jackson. He is undoubtedly lost without you."

After depositing Dulcie at Jackson's side, she made her way to the table, heavily laden with food. The best she could find was the champagne. She took up glass after glass until she had to sit for the bubbles filling her head. Another glass of champagne danced before her face. "May I offer you another?"

Caressa looked up to find Alexander Conrad, the Viscount of Godfrey and his two identical brothers weaving before her. "Wait, you do not have any brothers," she murmured.

The viscount laughed and sat next to her. "No, my dear, I don't." He reached for the champagne flute Caressa had taken from him. "Perhaps you have had enough?"

Caressa twisted away, ignoring the chill that washed over her glove as the cold liquid sloshed over the top and spilled over her. "Thank you, but I will keep it."

She tried to keep a note of primness in her voice but had to hold the glass with both hands to guide it to her lips. Still she felt some of the effervescent drink trickle from the corner of her mouth. She wiped the back of her already wet hand across her mouth. "Thank you."

The viscount smiled down at her, towering over her small form even when they both sat. "You look lovely today, my dear. While everyone else was watching the new marchioness, I had eyes only for you."

Caressa blushed and giggled. "Oh sir, you do flatter me."

"It is not vain flattery," he said in a low voice. The viscount brushed the backs of his fingers against her cheek and leaned forward.

A large hand wrapped around her upper arm. "Come along, Caressa."

She looked up into snapping green eyes. Kirkland's soft, generous mouth was pressed into a firm, unsmiling line. He pulled her up from her chair and out into the main hall. Once out of sight of those in the ballroom, Caressa tried wrenching her arm away from him. "Le'go o' me. Wha'd'you think you're doin'?"

"I am making certain you do not do anything to damage your person or your reputation." Kirkland spun her around to face him and the world around her wouldn't stop revolving. "Do you have any idea who you were speaking to? That was the Viscount of Godfrey. The man is known for turning innocents, such as yourself, into... into.... I can't even say it. As if that was not bad enough, he prefers to be more cruel than kind to his bed partners."

"Humbug. How coul'you poss'bly know?" Caressa's voice grated out of her throat. She wondered where the servants with the champagne had gone.

"Everyone knows!" He released her and paced away from her then back. "What is wrong, Caressa? You have been acting strangely for weeks. Ever since the Duke's Christmas gathering, you have been a different person. Where has our lovely little Caressa gone, hmm?"

Caressa felt herself hiccup as the first sobs came. Kirkland shushed her softly, crooning soft, murmuring sounds as he pulled her into his arms. She allowed it for all of a minute before she began beating on his shoulders and chest. Kirkland snuggled her tighter to his chest. "No, no, le' me go."

"Tell me what is wrong, Caressa. Please." One arm was wrapped like steel around her back. The hand of the other arm rubbed soothing circles over her back.

"What's so wrong with me, 'Land? Why don' you wan' me?" She continued to beat against his chest but her arms were losing strength while his single arm didn't seem to loosen even one little bit.

"What? What are you talking ab—" Caressa pushed herself up onto her toes and pressed her lips against his. She had seen couples kiss but had never allowed any of her suitors to kiss her; now she cursed her reticence. Perhaps if she had allowed one or two to steal a kiss, she would know what to do now. She tried to clear her mind, to remember what she had seen.

Caressa opened her lips and pulled Kirkland's lower lip into her mouth. She didn't know just what to do. Experimenting with this new experience, Caressa sucked on Kirkland's full, soft lower lip, lapped at it with her tongue, nipped with her teeth.

Kirkland gasped and pulled back from her. He stared deep into her eyes before threading his fingers into her hair and bringing his mouth down on hers. He thrust his tongue into her open mouth, brushed it against hers. Caressa felt as if her body had caught fire, moving from her lips to her breasts and lower.

Kirkland backed her into a dark corner. The arm banded around her slid free. His hand cupped her cheek, glided over her neck, and traced the lacy scooped neckline of her dress before settling on one breast. Caressa gasped as he massaged the small globe, rubbed her nipple.

His mouth left hers and followed the line of her chin, her throat. Caressa grabbed a hold of his head, pressing him close to her. His hand pulled the neckline of her dress, shift, and corset. When she felt his mouth close over her nipple, Caressa cried out. The heat of his mouth was intense. His teeth bit gently on the sensitive flesh.

Caressa gasped. She let her head fall back against the wall as she sighed and begged Kirkland to never stop.

"Caressa!" Her eyes snapped open at her mother's voice.

"Kirkland, let go of her this instant!" Kirkland's mother whispered vehemently.

Kirkland lifted his head and turned, keeping Caressa behind him. She looked around him but wasn't able to see very clearly. The sight wavered before her. The floor beneath her feet seemed to pitch back and forth like the deck of a ship.

"Kirkland, what are you doing to the Duke's daughter?" Lady Beatrice Perry demanded of her son.

"Your Grace, I am so sorry for my son's actions," Lord Konnor Perry uttered vehemently to the Duke of Courtney.

"No," Caressa slurred. "I did it." She scrambled out from behind Kirkland, her head protesting the movement. "I wanted him to touch me."

"Caressa! Be quiet you little fool!" Her mother came forward and yanked her away from Kirkland.

Caressa's head swam. "Mama, I do not feel well," she whispered seconds before her world faded to black.

Chapter Two

Kirkland leapt forward, catching Caressa in his arms. He gently lifted her into his arms, gazing into her beautiful face. All of the color had drained from it, leaving her stark white with rouged lips, looking like a child's doll.

There was a commotion at the doorway to the ballroom. Kirkland looked up to see the Duke and Duchess of Rothshire, closely followed by Dulcie and Jackson, coming toward them. Kirkland couldn't help but think how lovely Dulcie looked today. *Perhaps because she has just wed the man she loves,* some cruel voice whispered inside of his head.

Kirkland tore his gaze from her and returned his eyes to Caressa, feeling his conscience stab at him. He had just held Caressa against his body, taken liberties he had no right to take, and now he was mooning over Dulcie.

The smaller woman's words came back to him. *What's so wrong with me, 'Land? Why don' you wan' me,* she had demanded of him. He had no answer aside from that she wasn't Dulcie but he could not, *would* not say such hurtful words. He had known Caressa as long as he had known Dulcie. The little tow-headed sprite was his friend and he would not hurt her with such damning words.

Dulcie's father looked over the group gathered in the hall. "Into my study. We'll not parade Caressa in front of all of London." The Duke led the way, Kirkland immediately behind him.

When they all entered the room and the door was shut and locked, Kirkland breathed a sigh of relief on Caressa's behalf. He set her in one of the wingback chairs that faced one of the two large windows in the room. Dulcie, her mother, and Caressa's mother immediately swarmed around her. Jackson stood next to Dulcie, his hand rubbing her back in soothing circles.

Kirkland joined his father, Dulcie's father, and Caressa's father across the room. "Well," the Duke of Courtney said quietly, "what do you intend to do about my daughter, Perry?"

Kirkland opened his mouth but Konnor spoke up first. "Truly, Your Grace, my son is terribly sorry." When Kirkland remained silent, his father elbowed him in the ribs. "Are you not, boy?"

Kirkland looked to the chair in which Caressa sat. Her hand fluttered up and she sat forward, cradling her head in her hands. Was he terribly sorry? "Yes," he replied but wondered if it was the truth.

"There, you see? Now, why don't we give the dear girl a chance to rest before returning to the celebration," Konnor suggested.

Kirkland looked at Lord Davenport's face. He could see the man was not satisfied with his father's answer. Kirkland cleared his throat. "I will marry Caressa, if you would allow it."

The Duke and his father looked at Kirkland, his father aghast, Caressa's father looking relieved. "We will procure a special license first thing tomorrow morning," His Grace intoned.

Kirkland's eyes rounded as in dread. "A special license, Your Grace?"

"Yes. You have already been showing my daughter attention during the Season. Now, with this," the Duke waved a hand toward the door, "it will appear as though you are truly smitten and want to marry as soon as possible. I will request a special license from the Archbishop of Cantebury. Soon after, you two will be married and that will be the end of it."

Kirkland tried to swallow past the dryness in his throat. The idea that he would have more time to come to terms with the idea of having a marriage so much like his parents' was doused. Knowing it was the right thing to do, Kirkland nodded.

* * *

Kirkland's turned up his collar against the blustery wind as he, his father, and Davenport left the archbishop's office in Doctor's Commons. The duke carried the special license for which he had just paid thirty guineas. In six days, Caressa would be his wife.

Bile bit the back of his throat but Kirkland swallowed it down. It wasn't the thought of marrying Caressa that made him sick, but rather than taking time to choose which path he would take, which *wife* he would take, his grief and undeniable lust had chosen his path and his wife for him. He thought back on the morning of Dulcie and Jackson's wedding.

A well of protective anger had sprung to life in him when he had seen Godfrey poured over Caressa. He had extracted himself from a marriage minded mother and her too young daughter to rush to Caressa's rescue. When he had gotten her to the hall and she had turned a massive swirl of emotions on him, he had wanted to comfort her. Her lips on his had shocked him into stillness but her fiery passion had goaded him, flushed heat and lust through his body.

The events of the day had coalesced in that one moment and had blinded him to his actions. He had been guided by instinct. His cock had told him to take what comfort Caressa was offering. He wasn't angry with Caressa but with himself for allowing his control to break. He had never felt in such desperate need of completion as he had at that moment. What he was most surprised by was that it was a tiny little creature like Caressa that had brought him to his knees.

Chapter Three

Caressa sat in the drawing room with her mother, nervously awaiting Kirkland's arrival. Her brothers had been made to leave for White's earlier than they normally would have. Their parents didn't want to take the chance Henry and Geoffrey wouldn't make good on the threats to Kirkland's health they had been spouting since hearing of the events at Dulcie's wedding breakfast.

"Oh, good heavens!"

Caressa looked up at her mother's exclamation. The older woman was dabbing at her bodice with a napkin. "Mother?" Caressa giggled. She loved her with all her heart, but the woman had a tendency to be clumsy. "What happened?"

"Oh, bother. I accidentally tipped the cup before I had it at my lips and the damned thing was full."

Caressa giggled again at her mother's language. She excused herself to change her dress, leaving Caressa to let her mind wander more. She allowed it to wander to Kirkland, as it always inevitably did, and to her upcoming nuptials. As well as the upcoming wedding night.

A shiver ran through her when she remembered the feel of Kirkland's body against hers. Not many memories remained of Dulcie's wedding day, but Kirkland's kisses, his hands and mouth on her body, those broke through the drunken fog. She gasped at the ghost sensation of his lips sucking and his tongue flicking her nipple. Caressa held back a moan remembering the feel of his teeth gently nipping the sensitive peak.

"Caressa?" Kirkland's voice broke through her reverie. She looked up into his emerald eyes. "Are you all right? Your face is bright red."

Caressa swallowed. "Yes, I'm fine." Her voice practically wheezed past her lips. He took half a step toward her before backing away again. Color rose in Kirkland's cheeks and he looked down to his hands which were fidgeting with the brim of his tall hat. He hadn't removed his winter coat and his shoulders appeared rigid with unease under the thick wool.

The tension between them was an awkward thing. They had never been uncomfortable or at a loss of words when in one another's company. Now, the silence created a deafening buzz in Caressa's head. She wished she could reach out to him, touch him. She supposed in just a few more days, she would have the right and freedom to do so. The prospect terrified her nearly as much as it excited her.

Finally, her mother reappeared, a smile on her face. The older woman stepped ever so subtly into the space that separated Caressa from Kirkland. Not that there was a true reason for concern if Kirkland's disregard of her was any indication.

Caressa bit her lower lip hard before forcing a smile. At the front door, she and her mother donned their cloaks. Kirkland took them into town to see the Elgin marbles. It was almost warm and many people were entering the front doors of the British Museum to see the ancient Greek sculptures.

As Caressa walked down the packed aisles with Kirkland and her mother, Caressa's cheeks were on fire. The marbles depicted naked men and Centaurs, their genitals on display for all to ogle. Knowing it was shameful for her to think of such a thing, Caressa couldn't help but wonder if Kirkland looked like the marble illustrations. Caressa was overheated and short of breath by the time they reached the end and were able to leave.

Caressa was grateful for the cold air outside. It sucked the heat from her face, the cold likely nipping her skin as pink as her embarrassment had. Kirkland treated them to a small bite to eat at a nearby teahouse. Her mother dominated the conversation, which was fine by Caressa. Her mind continued to whirl around the marbles and Kirkland.

When he delivered them home, her mother invited Kirkland to stay for dinner. He respectfully declined, begging prearranged plans for the evening. Caressa escorted him to the door and looked up into his deep green eyes. The soft feel of Kirkland's fingertips grazing her face made Caressa's breath catch.

Kirkland pulled his hand away as though Caressa were on fire. He bowed over her hand, kissing the air above her knuckles before quickly straightening and leaving the house. He didn't look back, and Caressa felt disheartened and rejected.

Chest tightening, Caressa wondered why Kirkland hadn't begged off marrying her. Had he pushed, he would have been able to get out of it. Yes, it was true he had offered, but it had likely been no more than an automatic response brought on by years of training.

She could see it in the man's eyes, feel it in his touch that he had no interest in her. The thought of suffering a lifetime with the man she loved without his love in return terrified Caressa. She considered refusing to marry him, but realized that was something she didn't particularly care for. She was too selfish to turn him away. Her heart yearned for him and would not allow her to call off the wedding. There was nothing she could do but go on with the show.

*   *   *

The lights dimmed in the theater as the curtain rose to reveal a beautiful yet vicious young woman, Vitellia. Caressa loved *La Clemenza di Tito*. She loved the intrigue, the drama, and, of course, the benevolence of the wise Emperor Titus. For that matter, she loved Mozart's operas – even The Magic Flute. She argued that the Queen of the Night's maliciousness counteracted the romance, but secretively, she even loved the relationship between Tamino and Pamina.

Kirkland sat beside her. They were sitting behind their chaperones for the evening, Kirkland's parents, in one of the boxes of Her Majesty's Theatre. Looking at her intended, she noticed he was not paying attention to the opera. He had told her he had already attended an earlier performance, being an admirer of Mozart's, too.

It seemed odd to have known someone all her life, to have been in love with him for nearly as long, and to know so little of him. Turning her attention back to Vitellia and Sexto, she tried to concentrate on the characters. Unfortunately, they could not hold her attention.

As the handsome actor playing Titus walked onto the stage, Caressa looked back to Kirkland and reached over to lay her hand atop his. Kirkland looked down at their hands, turning his hand palm up and rubbing his fingertips over her gloved knuckles. Raising his eyes to her, Kirkland abruptly released her hand and returned his gaze to the wall at which he had been staring.

Caressa forced back the tears trying to slip free of her eyelids. She couldn't allow herself to cry, not while in Kirkland's presence. She couldn't allow him to see how deeply he was hurting her. She couldn't allow him to pity her.

Chapter Four

Three days later Caressa listened to a bishop friend of Kirkland's father as he droned out the wedding mass. It was Saturday afternoon, the end of January, dreary gray and bitterly cold outside. The special license her intended had obtained allowed for a later-in-the-day, private ceremony in the drawing room of her parent's London home. Not that the somber, sullen event was something Caressa would want to share with more than her family. Unfortunately, Dulcie had insisted she be allowed to attend.

I want to witness your happiest moment, Dulcie had said her voice gentle and loving as always. Had the circumstances been different, Caressa would have been more than happy to have Dulcie attend, but considering....

No! You will not think of it. You are marrying Kirkland today. Dulcie is married to Jackson. Dulcie is in love with Jackson and Kirkland knows that. You merely need to give him time. He will come around, Caressa. He just needs more than a week to do so.

Caressa squared her shoulders and listened intently to the bishop. She recited her vows; Kirkland recited his and placed her wedding ring on her finger. It wasn't a large diamond, but on her slim finger, it looked enormous. The platinum band fit just right on her finger. Earlier in the week, Caressa had noticed one of her rings had gone missing only to return Friday.

Caressa wondered which of her family members had smuggled the twined silver and rose gold ring to her fiancé. She looked to her oldest brother, Harry. Though he was mischievous, it was not likely something he would do. No, Harry would walk right up to her, lift her over his shoulder, and refuse to lower her until she gave him what he wanted.

Geoffrey might have. He had always known she had feelings for Kirkland and he approved because he knew Kirkland was a good man. Caressa also knew Geoffrey was observant enough to notice that, as good a man as her nearly-husband was, Kirkland was in love with another. It was even possible he intuited who Kirkland desired. Caressa didn't know if she could suffer seeing pity in her brother's eyes.

When the ceremony concluded and Kirkland pressed his lips chastely to her lips, Dulcie leapt to her feet, clapping. The others in the room, Jackson, Caressa's family and Kirkland's, followed suit. Forcing a strained smile to her face, Caressa signed the registry, followed by Kirkland and then Caressa's brothers. Caressa pressed a hand to her stomach, finding it odd that she was more nauseous now than she had been before the ceremony.

The wedding party adjourned to the dining room and Caressa sat across the table from her new husband. Her father had requested all of Caressa's favorite foods to be made and asked someone to fetch Maisy, Caressa's maid, to join them for the "splendid occasion." Around her was not the joyous celebration of Dulcie's wedding but a somber gathering of family and friends. It seemed more like a funeral rather than a wedding had just taken place.

Her elder brothers, Harry and Geoffrey, sat to her left. Harry, ever boisterous and cheerful, tried to pull everyone out of their quiet musings. He asked the footmen to bring more ale and wine, told his amusing tales of his times at school and on the continent, and congratulated Kirkland profusely for finally catching his baby sister. Geoffrey, quiet and studious, often elbowed their older brother, telling him to keep quiet. More than once Caressa caught Geoffrey looking away but she could see the concern in his eyes. Caressa sighed inwardly, knowing he felt the pity she had feared.

Dulcie patted her hand, startling Caressa out of her thoughts. Her friend leaned over to whisper, "Are you all right?"

Caressa saw the genuine love and concern in her friend's gaze. Caressa summoned as bright a smile as she could muster. "Yes, why wouldn't I be?"

Dulcie sighed sadly and sat back in her chair. Caressa knew her friend wished she would speak honestly but what could she say? Caressa was married to the man she loved but he didn't love her. She wondered, when he touched her, would he be thinking of

Dulcie? Imagining her friend's coppery hair, her full curves? She had half of what she wanted and would have to learn to live her life contentedly with only Kirkland's ring and not his heart.

When supper ended, the women followed Caressa upstairs to her childhood bedroom, the room she and Kirkland would share on their first night as husband and wife. Her mother and new mother-in-law helped her undress and put on a new white night rail they had purchased for her trousseau. She asked the older women to leave, leaving her alone with Dulcie.

Dulcie sat her at the room's small vanity, unpinned her hair, and brushed the long blond locks.

"Dulcie, is it truly as horrible as my grandmothers have always told me?"

Caressa watched her friend's reflection, noting the blush that crept up Dulcie's chest, neck, then face. "N-no, it is not horrible." Dulcie cleared her throat before continuing. "The first time can be frightening and there is a little pain, however, you can receive enjoyment as well as your husband."

"My husband Kirkland," Caressa said, looking for Dulcie's reaction. She wanted to see for herself how her friend felt about her marriage to Kirkland.

As one would always expect of Dulcie, she smiled without jealousy or malice. It was the same smile she had always been so quick to give – one full of love and warmth. "Yes, your husband Kirkland."

Dulcie set down the hairbrush and pulled Caressa to her feet over to the bed. "Are you happy, Caressa?"

Caressa nodded. "Of course. I have always wanted to have Kirkland, now he is mine."

Again, Caressa looked for Dulcie's reaction. Her friend pulled her into a hug. "Good. I only want for you to find the happiness I have found with Jackson."

Caressa heard the truth and sincerity in her friend's words. She smiled for Dulcie's benefit, knowing she'd likely never be truly happy. Kirkland did not want her – he wanted the woman sitting beside her.

There was a knock at the door and Dulcie stood. "Are you ready?"

"As ready as I will ever be." Caressa took several deep breaths, holding each for a moment before releasing the air.

Dulcie walked to the door and opened it. Kirkland stood on the other side of the threshold. He looked at Dulcie first and in his gaze Caressa could see yearning. Dulcie did not notice for she was smiling encouragement to Caressa. Kirkland stepped into the room and Dulcie quietly excused herself.

The only sound in the room was the crackling of the fire that had been built in the small fireplace across the room from her bed. Caressa looked on as her new husband walked to the other side of the bed and undressed in preparation for bed. When he stripped off his shirt, Caressa bit her lip in wonder. His chest and belly looked strong, defined by muscle, tanned as though he spent much time in the sun without one of his finely made shirts to protect him from browning. Kirkland didn't immediately remove his breeches but instead pulled a long night shirt from one of the leather trunks that had been stowed in her room before the ceremony. Turning his back on her, he donned the nightshirt and finished undressing.

When he slipped under the blankets, Caressa's breath caught at how large he looked. While her delicate looking brass bed was large enough to accommodate two, Kirkland took up more than half and he looked thoroughly god-like, huge and floating on a cloud of white and gold.

Caressa quickly joined him, nervous and excited and scared and near to desperation to feel his touch. She stayed still, lying on her back, waiting – hoping – Kirkland would turn to her. Minutes went by as she waited until she no longer could. She turned to her side to face him and found him already asleep. Tears burned her eyes.

Caressa lifted his arm gently and curled around him. At least if he was asleep she could cuddle to his side as she cried without him being able to deny her.

Chapter Five

Kirkland kept his eyes closed. When he had felt Caressa's small hands pull his arm away from his side, he had wondered what she was about. Then she wrapped herself around him and he felt as her tears wetted the linen of his nightshirt. He didn't know what had made her cry but it tore him apart. He hated that his friend was so sad. *She is not just my friend anymore. Now she is my wife and it is my duty to stop her tears.*

Kirkland rolled gently to his side and pulled her against his chest, cradling the back of her head in one hand. "Shh, Caressa. I know this isn't what we wanted, but we will make the best of it, hmm?"

Caressa pulled back from him and looked into his eyes. She didn't speak, merely looked at him before wrapping one of her own small hands around his neck and pulling his lips toward hers.

Wanting to comfort her, comfort himself, Kirkland dipped his head and gently kissed Caressa's lips. When she opened her mouth and her tongue swept his lips, Kirkland could not help but respond. He touched his tongue to hers and groaned. He explored her mouth, the wet velvet feel of her tongue against his, the sharpness of her teeth, the softness of the inside of her cheeks, the hard, ridged roof of her mouth.

Caressa tugged his hand away from her head, dragged it down until he cupped her breast. His cock hardened as he gently massaged the small globe. He scraped his fingernail across the fabric covered nipple and she shivered and moaned.

When Kirkland pulled his lips away from Caressa's, she began whispering to him. Whispering words no genteel lady should use. But as she begged, Kirkland's body tightened and his erection turned painful.

"Please, Kirkland, I need you. Kiss me. Touch me between my legs. I need to feel you... everywhere. Touch me everywhere. Please," Caressa gasped into his ear.

This isn't right, Kirkland thought through his haze of lust. He shouldn't be taking advantage of Caressa like this. They were both distraught. If he hadn't touched her at Dulcie's wedding brunch, they wouldn't have had to marry.

Difficult though it was, Kirkland pulled away. Covering her breast, he looked deep into her clear blue eyes. "I'm sorry, Caressa. I shouldn't be forcing myself on you. It is the stress of the day – of having to marry."

The look on her face was one of horrified dismay. He pulled Caressa's arms from around his neck, gently kissed her forehead, and turned to his side, facing away from her. After a short while, he heard her begin to cry, the sound muffled as though she had turned her face into her pillow. His attack on her body must have finally breached her shock. Kirkland only hoped she would forgive him in time.

*   *   *

Caressa awoke before Kirkland. Her eyes still stung from crying herself to sleep. She had offered herself to her new husband, offered herself wantonly – hungrily. And he had turned away from her. She could not face him this morning.

Throwing her heavy robe over her shoulders, Caressa grabbed up a shift, corset, and dress and quietly left the room. She knew which room Dulcie and Jackson were sleeping in and hastily made her way there. Jackson answered her frantic knocking dressed in only undone trousers and an untucked linen shirt.

The expression on his face was thunderous until he looked at her. His face melted from anger to concern. He pulled her into the room. "Dulcie, something is wrong."

Dulcie stepped out from behind a dressing screen, she herself in a heavy robe to ward off the winter's cold. She looked worriedly at Caressa. "Caressa? What is the matter?"

Tears gathered and again spilled down her cheeks. Caressa had been so certain she had cried herself dry the night before. Evidently, she could cry oceans where Kirkland was concerned.

Jackson walked to his wife and gathered the rest of his clothing for the day. He whispered something to Dulcie and lightly kissed her lips. He left the room without a word to Caressa but with a gentle pat on her shoulder.

Dulcie hurried to her side and guided her to the bed. As they sat on the edge, Caressa cried on her friend's shoulder, hiccupping her way through the previous night's events, though she did not go into detail of what Kirkland did to her body. "It was h-horrible. It h-hurt s-s-so much when he t-turned from me. My heart shattered!"

"Shh, it will be all right, love," Dulcie crooned. "Wait and see. Kirkland was likely terrified he would hurt you. Perhaps he was embarrassed to make love to you in your parents' home. I'm certain everything is fine."

Caressa doubted Dulcie was correct but did not doubt her friend's sincerity. She would wait. What else cold she do?

They stayed on the edge of the bed until Caressa's tears stopped. Her throat felt raw. Her eyes felt as though someone had kicked sand into her face. When she felt under control, Dulcie helped Caressa into her corset and traveling dress. She didn't feel she could face one of the maids, especially knowing they would see the lack of evidence of a marriage night coupling when they cleaned the room later.

As she pulled the laces on Dulcie's half -corset, Caressa saw in her mind's eye the kiss her friend had shared with Kirkland. She yanked on the strings, causing Dulcie to gasp.

"Caressa, I believe that is tight enough." Dulcie's voice was breathless.

Caressa gasped and loosened the corset strings so that her friend could breathe. She apologized profusely but Dulcie waved off her words, telling Caressa she knew Caressa was in poor spirits and distracted. Caressa's face heated. Why did Dulcie have to be so understanding?

Once they were finished dressing, the two women entered the hallway to find their husbands waiting on them. Jackson walked up to Dulcie, taking her hand and kissing her knuckles courteously. It seemed a gentlemanly gesture but Caressa could see the wicked sparkle in Jackson's eyes as he looked at his wife. Dulcie must have seen it, too, for she blushed and smiled at her husband.

Caressa turned to Kirkland. He was turned away from the scene before them. Sighing inwardly, Caressa walked to him and wrapped her arm around his. Kirkland looked at her, a dull shine in his eyes. He patted her hand and escorted her downstairs and to the dining room where their families awaited them.

After a light, quiet breakfast, Caressa, Kirkland and his family, and Dulcie and Jackson set off for Lord and Lady Perry's estate, Lynwood Hall. The Baron's estate was closest. They would have lunch there before Dulcie and Jackson would set off for Torningate.

Caressa felt tears threaten as she hugged her mother and father then each of her brothers. She was leaving one of the homes she had known since the day she was born. After spending the night at Lynwood Hall, Kirkland and Caressa would set out for a wedding trip to his father's hunting lodge further north of the estate.

An arm wrapped around each of her brother's necks, Caressa told them both to behave. She prayed all would be well with them. While Harry was all too likely to get some unfortunate girl with child, she feared Geoffrey's social ineptitude would continue to hinder his success in finding a wife. She wished she could be close by to help both of them, but now she was off to an uncertain future.

Caressa climbed into the carriage and stared out the window, watching first the city then the countryside roll past them. She refused to let the despair she could feel threatening flood through her. If nothing else, she had married the man she loved. After a time, he would grow to see her as a woman. As his woman, Caressa hoped.

Chapter Six

Lynwood Hall was an enormous Georgian manor house. Much of the first floor interior reflected the Egyptian décor so popular among the ton. Obelisks, canopic jars, and even a small replica of the Great Sphinx decorated the front parlor. A golden statue of a cat with a collar of ruby enamel disks and diamond-shaped eyes of sapphire blue enamel sat atop a table serving as an oil lamp.

Kirkland asked Bowers, the butler, to see after their friends before he personally escorted Caressa up to his apartments. His rooms were appointed much more simply, but, in Caressa's opinion, more comfortably. The colors were all very masculine with dark greens and blues dominating the space.

He opened the door to his bedchamber – *their* bedchamber – and her eyes rounded at the size of his four poster bed. The massive mahogany pillars and slabs that framed the bed, broken only by the heavy green velvet drapes that gathered at the end of each of the rods that connected the posters at the top, made her feel small as a babe. There was little doubt in her mind that Dulcie would feel so intimidated. She reckoned five people could easily sleep in the bed and do so without complaint.

That thought made Caressa's cheeks burn. She wondered if her husband had ever truly put the size to use. More heat infused her face. Caressa ducked her head and preceded Kirkland into the bedroom. He guided her to a bureau atop which sat a basin and a steaming pitcher of water, face towels folded neatly beside them. "You can wash up here. I was told your personal maid and belongings have arrived from your father's estate. I will have her sent in to help you change out of your traveling clothes."

He turned her by the shoulders and tilted her face up to his. "It will be all right, Caressa. We'll make the best of things, hmm?"

Caressa gave a watery smile and nodded, knowing she would do all in her power to make more than the best of their situation. Kirkland smiled down at her and kissed her forehead before leaving her alone in the room.

Scrubbing the tears she refused to let fall from her eyes, Caressa removed her jacket. Steam wafted into her face as she poured hot water into the basin. The door opened behind her.

"Miss Caressa! How are you, deary?"

Maisy, her maid since childhood, picked her way to Caressa. She watched the older woman look around cautiously. Having known each other for so long, Caressa knew her maid was not entirely comfortable in new situations. Until Maisy was more comfortable at Lynnwood Hall, she would be stepping carefully, watching closely, even breathing shallowly if she must.

Caressa smiled bravely. "I am wonderful, Maisy."

Her maid turned wide, owl eyes on her and smiled in return. "Finally landed yourself that fine young man, my lady. You must feel wonderful."

Caressa felt her smile slip a little. She nodded and turned back to the basin. She dampened a cloth and lifted it to her face.

"Here, now, Miss. You are going to ruin your fine clothes. Here, let us get those off of you while you refresh yourself. I will choose something suitable for you to wear to dinner with your husband's family." Maisy helped her undress down to her shift, chuckling over Dulcie's efforts of securing Caressa's demi-corset. She imagined her friend would hear similar chuckling from her maid as their knots were more artful than useful.

Once Caressa was clean to her satisfaction without benefit of a tub, Maisy helped her dress in a lovely rose colored muslin dress. The sleeves skimmed down her arms, the neckline, while demure enough, still left much of her upper chest exposed. Her maid pinned her hair to allow tendrils of her curling blond tresses to fall and frame her face.

Stepping into her slippers, Caressa prayed she did nothing that night to embarrass herself in front of her new husband's family. Kirkland awaited her in the sitting area of his – *their* – suite. She felt a sense of pride when his eyes widened as he looked at her. She smiled. Kirkland's Adam's apple bobbed as he swallowed.

Kirkland escorted her down stairs and into the long formal dining room. His family, Dulcie and Jackson poured into the room behind them. The cook and her kitchen staff had prepared a large, elaborate supper with mutton, pheasant, and roast pork. Every vegetable imaginable filled bowls and platters and all smelled delicious.

This evening's meal was less strained than the previous night's. There was quiet but happy talk around the table. Beatrice asked after Dulcie's new niece and when she and Jackson were planning on giving her cousins. Caressa saw, from the corner of her eye, Kirkland blanch.

Dulcie blushed and Jackson chuckled. "We plan to wait for a short while," he said.

When Lady Perry began to admonish them lightly, Kirkland cleared his throat. "Mother, if they want to wait, they may wait. You are neither Dulcie's nor Jackson's mother. Stop badgering them." He took a long swallow of his wine and signaled for more from the footman.

Caressa ducked her head, feeling her cheeks heat in mortification as the dining room fell silent. She could feel eyes on her. Lifting her chin just a little, she looked though her lashes. Her friend looked somewhat flabbergasted at Kirkland's outburst.

Trying to dispel the tension suddenly filling the room, Jackson said lightly, "That's right, Kirkland. Shouldn't you be needling your son for grandchildren, my lady? What fine children they will make, I daresay."

Caressa cut her eyes back to her husband to see him staring, almost aghast, at their friend. She had trouble swallowing around the lump in her throat and she picked up her wine glass, hoping to dislodge it. The alcohol burned her throat and she gasped and coughed.

Kirkland clapped her lightly on the back. "Are you all right, Caressa?"

She looked up into his eyes, seeing concern but not the strong emotions she saw in Jackson's eyes when he looked at Dulcie. She supposed choking on a bit of wine wouldn't normally inspire such a look, but she had never seen Jackson without that loving glint in his eyes. She wanted that look from her husband. Caressa didn't want Kirkland to think of her as only his friend, but as his lover, his love.

"I – no, I'm not feeling very well. I think I would like to go upstairs and lie down, now. If everyone would excuse me?" She rose to her feet, purposefully swaying slightly so that Kirkland would reach for her.

"Come along, Caressa. I will take you upstairs so that you may rest."

Seeing this as an opportunity to angle her husband into bed, she plotted as Kirkland guided her back to their suite and into the bedroom across the suite from the one he had shown her to when they'd arrived. The furniture was smaller, almost delicate – more like the furniture in her rooms at home.

Noticing her trunks and several of her larger possessions around the room, Caressa was confused but decided her seduction of her husband could easily begin here. Caressa crossed the threshold and began to unpin her hair. She looked over her shoulder at Kirkland. He stood outside the room, watching her.

"Would you help me undress, Kirkland?"

He shifted from foot to foot. "I will – ahem – I will ring for Maisy to help you." Kirkland entered the room, heading for the bell pull that hung down one wall.

Caressa stepped in front of him. "Please, Kirkland, you are here. It will take Maisy time to get here, if she doesn't get lost in the unfamiliar house. I am tired and would like to go to bed." She stepped closer, so close the tips of her breasts brushed his chest. Caressa looked up at him through her lashes. "Please Kirkland," she whispered.

He took a deep breath and faced her away from him. His gentle fingers released the hooks and ties along her back. Caressa shivered as Kirkland's fingers brushed her skin as he pushed the thick fabric over her shoulders and down her arms.

She could hear his breath rasping in and out of his mouth. He tugged the ties of her corset to release her from the confining material. She breathed a sigh of relief as he pulled the stiff garment from her. She felt him step away, the loss of his heat sending a chill across her back. Caressa turned to her husband. His deep green eyes trailed down her length and she wondered what he could see of her through the shift shielding her nude body.

When his eyes returned to hers, she swore they sparked with a heat with which she sincerely wanted to warm herself. He coughed into his hand and turned his gaze from her. "Is there any other way I can assist you?"

Caressa decided to see if the sparks of attraction she had seen in his eyes could be turned into an inferno. She stepped up to Kirkland and placed her hand in the center of his chest. He looked at her and she saw again the way his eyes widened and the green was almost eliminated by black.

Caressa slid her fingers down and over the thick fabric of his vest and dinner jacket. She slowly worked at the buttons. Kirkland stood motionless, looking at her as she stared into his eyes. He was running his gaze all over her. When his eyes stopped on her mouth, Caressa licked her lips.

Kirkland groaned and brought his mouth down on hers. Caressa eagerly met his kiss. His firm lips were warm and smooth. He sucked her bottom lip into his mouth and skimmed his velvety tongue along the sensitive skin. Caressa gasped and worked faster at removing Kirkland's clothing.

She had finished with his jacket and was now unfastening the last button on his vest. Kirkland shrugged out of them, throwing them to the floor before gathering Caressa into his arms. His tongue rubbed against hers and Caressa felt herself growing lightheaded. She needed him.

The thin fabric of her shift tightened around her waist. She felt his hands drag the material up her body until he had to pull away from her lips to pull the shift over her head. His eyes once again traveled down her body. Gentle fingers followed his gaze.

Caressa's breath hitched when his gentle touch brushed one of her nipples. She held back a small giggle as his fingers glided over the sensitive skin of her stomach. However, she could not contain the moan as he sifted through the hair over her mound. He slid his fingers between her thighs and pressed the longest against her. A sob tore from her throat when he rubbed a delicious, tingling spot. It was so pleasurable it almost hurt.

Kirkland continued to circle his fingertip over the spot, making the pleasure and pain mount higher and higher. Caressa clawed at his shirt and the buttons on his trousers. His hands left her body to finish undressing himself. When he was bare, Kirkland pulled Caressa into his arms once again. One of his large hands curled around the back of her neck as the other traced down her spine and pressed her body to his.

Caressa gasped at the hard, searing hot length of his member pressing into her belly. Her fingers clutched his shoulders, scraped at his back, squeezed the hard globes of his rear. She pressed against Kirkland, her hips twitching in time to the throbbing low in her belly.

He lifted her in his arms and carried her to the bed. Caressa held out her arms to Kirkland and he laid the length of his body along hers. Instinctively, Caressa's legs fell open to cradle Kirkland's body between her thighs. Kirkland pressed his sex against hers, thrust the length of himself against the delicious spot he had been rubbing only moments ago. Caressa whimpered and clasped Kirkland's hips with her legs.

Tremors started in her womb. They turned into flames that quickly engulfed her entire body. Caressa cried out and clawed at the strong muscles of Kirkland's back as her body shook hard. Kirkland pulled his hips back and thrust forward, his body invading hers. She cried out as pain burned away the last of her pleasure and she tried to crawl away from him, but Kirkland wouldn't allow it.

He stayed inside her, not moving his hips at all. His large hands clasped her head as he brought his down for a kiss. His tongue forged deeply but gently into her mouth. Kirkland's tongue rubbed against Caressa's, making her shiver. He nibbled her lips, making them feel swollen, making her want more.

His lips left hers and skimmed down her chin, the soft skin underneath. Down the length of her neck and across her collarbone. Kirkland nuzzled his nose in the valley between her small breasts and licked the sensitive skin, making Caressa sigh.

When the wet heat of his mouth engulfed her nipple, she gasped and buried her hands in his hair. He sucked hard and began to move his hips. Caressa shuddered at the feel of him dragging out of her body and sliding back into her. His sharp teeth nipped the tip of her nipple before he soothed the pleasurable pain with his velvety tongue.

Sighing, Caressa lifted her hips to meet Kirkland's. His hands clasped her hips and pinned them to the bed. He looked up into her eyes, his mouth still around her nipple, and he slowly shook his head. Kirkland sucked hard as he pulled his head away from her breast. He moved to her other breast, lovingly torturing it as had the first.

Kirkland pushed in and ground his groin against her. The motion brushed that spot again and Caressa felt herself begin to shake all over again. He moved slowly in and out of her, pulling the shattering sensation from her. Caressa wrapped her legs around Kirkland's waist, begging for more. Kirkland thrust harder until Caressa heard the slap of his skin against hers.

A scream ripped from her throat, the feeling rolling through her was so intense it caused shards of light to explode behind her eyes. Kirkland groaned, "Caressa, oh Caressa." She felt his body go rigid above her.

Completely spent, Caressa's arms and legs slithered from around Kirkland. Never had she felt anything so wonderful. Kirkland rolled to the bed beside Caressa and pulled her to his side. She looked into his face, reaching for a kiss. A soft snore rumbled from his throat. He was asleep.

Caressa laughed and snuggled down against his chest. She would get her kiss in the morning.

Chapter Seven

Caressa woke to the sweet and savory smells of breakfast and the soft tinkling of china against silver as a maid carried a tray, heavy with food and juice, into the bedroom. A smile curled her lips and she rolled her head only to find Kirkland gone from her bed. She told herself not to be hurt. He likely had some business he needed to attend to early this morning before they set off on their trip.

Caressa ate her breakfast before washing up and allowing Maisy and the other maids to dress her and fix her hair. She hoped wherever Kirkland was that he returned quickly so that they could leave soon. However, when she arrived downstairs, she found her new husband. He was bending over Dulcie's hand, brushing her knuckles with his lips.

Dulcie looked up at her. "Caressa! You're finally awake!"
Her friend's full mouth tipped into a smile. She pulled away from Kirkland and came to Caressa.

Caressa saw Kirkland look at her quickly, his cheeks taking on a faint blush before turning back to Jackson and talking to the Marquis in quiet tones. Swallowing her disappointment, Caressa smiled at Dulcie, giving her lifelong friend a hug. "I'm sorry we must leave so early this morning," Dulcie apologized. "We promised Jackson's parents we would be back in time to see them off. They are going to the Orient." Dulcie laughed. "If I know his mother, she will bring back toys for grandchildren she doesn't even have yet."

Caressa laughed and smiled warmly. She was so happy for Dulcie. Her friend had been terrified her husband's parents would hear about what had happened between Dulcie and Jackson before they had married and would not want their son to marry her. Dulcie had been very wrong. Jackson's parents, the Duke and Duchess of

Waterton, loved Dulcie. They had long known of their son's intentions to marry Dulcie and had encouraged him to offer for her for years.

Now, if only Caressa could turn Kirkland's head as Dulcie did. She had often been envious of her friend's voluptuous figure. Now her jealousy was strengthened by her husband's reaction to Dulcie. She surreptitiously compared her small breasts to Dulcie's larger ones and wondered if they were what made the difference to Kirkland.

Unfortunately, there was nothing to be done about her child-like body. Caressa bit the inside of her cheek and forced herself not to cry and to smile up at Dulcie. "I am so happy you could be with me," she whispered to her friend.

"I am so happy you allowed me to come," Dulcie replied. "I wish the two of you all of the happiness in the world."

They hugged again and Caressa looked over at her husband, watching Kirkland watch them. She wondered if she and Kirkland would be able to find happiness. Maybe even... love?

*   *   *

Kirkland looked on as Dulcie and Caressa spoke in low tones at the foot of the grand staircase. His cheeks still burned at Caressa finding him bent over Dulcie's hand. He supposed it was more guilt than embarrassment he felt. While it wasn't out of the question, and was even expected, to brush one's lips across the air over a lady's knuckles, Kirkland was fair to certain he had more than touched his lips to her skin. Kirkland was afraid he had been caught by Caressa practically devouring Dulcie's hand.

"Kirkland?"

He looked to his friend Jackson. He cleared his throat. "Thank you for coming to the ceremony. I know it meant very much to Caressa. I'm just sorry it cut short your own wedding trip."

"Nonsense. Dulcie and I wouldn't have missed it for anything. Had I even suggested such a thing, she'd have likely had my head for it," Jackson chuckled.

Even as he forced the words past the lump in his throat, he forced his jaw, neck, and shoulders to loosen. Kirkland felt ready to break. The week had been more than difficult. First, he'd had to watch the woman he wanted marry another man. Then, he had forced himself into a marriage that mirrored that of his parents.

He told himself Dulcie was better off with Jackson. They loved each other madly, had been destined for one another. He also told himself it wasn't Caressa's fault she wasn't Dulcie.

Kirkland felt as though he should be strung up by his toes. It was unfair to Caressa to wish she was someone else. Caressa was a gentle, kind woman. She was worthy of more than a husband who looked at her and pictured rich copper hair in place of her thick golden tresses. A man wishing for light brown eyes rather than deep blue ones. Part of Kirkland had always felt Dulcie's deliciously curved body could better withstand his passion than any other lady of the *ton*. However, last night in Caressa's bed, he found a very compatible bed partner.

If nothing else, he and Caressa would have a fine marriage after dark. He had been pleasantly surprised by how excitable his little bride had been. As she had scratched her sharp little nails along his skin, trails of fire had burned in their wake. The way she had responded to his control over her had fed the desire he had been surprised to feel for her.

It made him think back on the day of Dulcie and Jackson's wedding. He had sought comfort in Caressa's arms. Even knowing she had been too inebriated to defend herself against his advances, Kirkland hadn't been able to stop himself from taking her in his arms. He wondered what he would have done to her had their parents not arrived in the hallway to find him manhandling her.

He thought of her words to him that day. *What is so wrong with me, Kirkland?* He still did not understand. Men had approached her parents since prior to her first Season but they had always declined their offers. Why would they do that to her? Did her parents not wish for her to marry? Did they only agree to her and Kirkland's union due to the circumstances?

These questions weighed heavily on Kirkland's mind. Caressa was a lovely woman. She was sweet, intelligent, talented, and he now knew she was passionate. The only reason for her to have gone unmarried as long as she had could be her parents. But why?

He sighed. It no longer mattered. She had been forced to wed Kirkland and now they must make the best of the situation. He would continue to bed her until she got with child. Once he had an heir, he would no longer need to trouble her at night.

Kirkland turned back to Jackson who was chuckling and looking at him with a devilish light in his eyes. "Can hardly wait to be rid of us, eh?"

"Pardon?" Kirkland asked, confused.

"With the way you are looking at your bride, I would imagine you are ready for us to leave so that you may take her back to your suite and make the most of your time." Jackson clapped him on his back and Kirkland issued a noncommittal murmur.

The women joined them at the front entrance, arms linked together. Both women were scarlet with tears in their eyes and the hiccupping remains of giggles on their lips. "I suppose we had best be on our way, husband. Your parents will never forgive us if we are not there to say goodbye." Dulcie hugged Caressa one last time and walked to Jackson, the look of love heavy in her eyes.

Kirkland held out his arm for Caressa and she slipped her hand through the bend at his elbow. They followed their friends outside and waved to them as their carriage took them away from the manor house. Once inside again, Kirkland kissed the back of Caressa's hand. "You will have to excuse me for a short while, Caressa. My father requires my help on some business. I will return shortly then we can be on our way."

Kirkland left Caressa in the entryway and headed for his father's office. Truthfully, there was no emergency, but he felt the need to get away from Caressa. He was certain she wanted to talk to him, maybe even shout at him, about what she had seen when she had arrived downstairs. She had every right to be angry. How embarrassed she must have been.

Kirkland had to learn to control himself. He owed it to Caressa to be more respectful to her. He knew men who did not care for the hearts of their wives and intendeds. They humiliated the women in their lives at every turn all because they could. Though Kirkland did not fool himself that this marriage was a love match, he cared very much for Caressa. If nothing else, they were friends. She deserved to be treated with respect.

He had to let go of his foolish desire for Dulcie. He had known for a very long time she and Jackson would be married, had even deterred other potential suitors. There had been one fleeting moment when it looked as though Kirkland could have her, but one kiss had told him it was not meant to be.

Tonight, he would join Caressa in her bed once again. At least there was heat between them in bed. If that was all they had, so be it.

Chapter Eight

Caressa watched her husband's retreating form. Once he was out of sight, she climbed the stairs and returned to their suite. When she had seen him kissing Dulcie's hand, Caressa had felt sick. She wanted her husband to lavish attention upon her, not Dulcie, nor any other woman! Caressa decided she would seduce him.

She had asked Dulcie if she knew of anything she could do for her husband. As Dulcie proceeded to describe things she could do *with* Kirkland and *to* Kirkland, Caressa's heart had begun to race. In her mind, she had been able to see herself perform all of the acts Dulcie had described.

She looked through her armoire, pulling out all of the lovely nightgowns her mother had picked out for her months ago. Every new Season her mother insisted on buying her a new trousseau. Now she would finally be able to wear these lovely items of sheer and lacy gowns. She looked them over critically. Some were too young, meant for the girls who had only now been presented at court. One, though beautiful, was entirely too daring, even to wear when alone, let alone in the company of one's husband.

She settled on a gown with a sheer cream back and skirt and pale green lace bodice. The back was laced with a wide cream satin ribbon. The sleeves were long but slit the entire length with only a single tie at the elbow. She placed it as well as the rest of her trousseau into one of the bags being brought to the hunting lodge.

They left not long after Dulcie and Jackson, riding north. Sitting on the bench across from her new husband, Caressa snuggled under the blanket she pulled up to her chin and rubbed her feet over the heated brick under them. She watched the man she loved as he seemed to forget she was in the carriage with him.

Kirkland was absorbed, writing in a journal. It made Caressa think of her brothers and their grand tales of devilishness. She knew much of Harry's and Geoffrey's stories were just that – stories – but she loved to listen and laugh over them, anyhow.

She had once suggested they turn the tales into stories to be published. Her father had laughed, saying that wasn't a proper past time for the sons of a duke. It was strange, thinking back on that day. She could have sworn Geoffrey had lit up just a tiny bit at the thought, his face falling when their father had rebuffed the idea.

Recently she had come across her brother writing furiously. She had entered the library of their London home and he had been sitting at the desk, which was against a wall of windows. She had tiptoed up behind him but he had swiftly flipped the papers over and told her she would be punished for spying. He had chased her around the house and out the kitchen door. He had also ruined one of her favorite dresses when he'd knocked her into the fountain in the center of the garden. She smiled, remembering how she had insisted he help her out – when he had reached in for her, Caressa had yanked on Geoffrey's hand, unbalancing him into the water, too. They had laughed until their parents and brother had come out and found them. Their mother had stood there admonishing them. Their father, though he had a stern look in his eyes, had been holding his hand over his mouth to stop his laughter. Harry had been quite annoyed that he had missed the fun. Even the memory nearly had Caressa choke with laughter.

Kirkland looked up from the leather-bound pages but Caressa merely shook her head at the question in his eyes. "Just reminiscing." Clearing her throat, she stretched her neck in the direction of Kirkland and his book. "What are you writing?"

Kirkland looked tiredly at the paper. "I am writing down some notes for a meeting my father and I must attend in London when you and I return to Lynwood Hall. An old business partner of his has been trying to undermine investors' confidence in Father's capabilities. We are meeting with the biggest of the investors to settle their fears."

Caressa nodded and stretched forward trying to see the notebook. The carriage hit a rut throwing Caressa into Kirkland's chest. The book tumbled from her husband's lap as he reached for her. His arms closed around her, holding Caressa tight to his chest. "Are you all right?"

Looking into Kirkland's glass-green eyes, Caressa felt her blood race as memories of the night before crashed around in her head. Caressa grasped his shoulders and stretched up, pressing her lips to Kirkland's.

At first, his lips remained pressed together. But then she laced her fingers through his hair, upsetting the flat topped hat he wore, and tickled his lips with the tip of her tongue. A growl vibrated against Caressa's lips before her husband invaded her mouth.

Pushing her skirt up to her hips, Kirkland pulled her astride his lap, leaving her legs and rear vulnerable to the chilled air in the carriage. His hands rubbed roughly down her thighs until he cupped her knees. Using the pad of his thumbs to rub small circles into the tender flesh covering the muscles of her inner thighs, Kirkland slowly petted his way to her dampening core.

Caressa whimpered against Kirkland's mouth as he gently rubbed the surface of her nether-lips. The hair covering her mound twisted and pulled making her hips jerk involuntarily. Kirkland's thumbs breeched her and he pressed hard against that sensitive, tender spot he had manipulated the night before.

Wrapping her arms tightly around Kirkland's shoulders, Caressa pressed her chest against her husband's, trying to alleviate the ache in her neglected nipples. She's had no idea prior to her first night with Kirkland just how sensitive the innocuous little buds could be. Now that Kirkland had shown her the pleasure to be had by their manipulation, Caressa was greedy for more.

Kirkland released her mouth to tilt his head at a new angle and took her lips again. Caressa gasped as he rubbed deep and hard with both his tongue and his thumbs. Lower belly tightening, tingle rushing through her legs, Caressa moved her hips backward and forward. As Kirkland pressed one thumb deep inside her body, Caressa came, crying her completion into her husband's mouth as the exquisite and frightening sensation rolled through her.

After her body melted against his in utter contentment, Kirkland removed his hands from her thighs and lifted her to reposition her across his lap. He readjusted her dress before pulling over her the blanket she had lost when thrown into his arms.

Drowsiness pulled at Caressa's eyelids. She fought to keep her eyes open, wanting to spend this quiet, perfect moment with Kirkland. He must have noticed her drifting off, though, for he kissed her eyes closed. "Go ahead and sleep, 'Ressa," he murmured. "We still have hours to ride before we arrive."

Nodding against this shoulder, Caressa let herself drift off even as a part of her brain told her not to succumb. Her mind tried to remind her of the hard shaft pressed against her hip, but the lure of rest was too much. Sleep pulled her under, Kirkland's arms wrapped around her.

*   *   *

Kirkland and the carriage driver carried in the few items he and Caressa had brought with them to the lodge. Caressa was warming herself by the fire he had set first thing upon their arrival. Once everything had been unloaded and taken into the lodge, Kirkland dismissed the carriage driver who told them he would return for them in a week.

Kirkland heard Caressa sigh, though the sound wasn't very loud. He didn't feel she was trying to show her disappointment in him but he couldn't help but feel responsible for the tiny sound. He knew a week wasn't much time, but he needed to return to business sooner than he might have had to, given more time to prepare.

I did the right thing. I did the only thing I could do. Kirkland had told himself those words every day for the past week. The words were true, but he didn't like the way they made him sound a martyr. That wasn't fair to Caressa. And if the previous night was any indication, marriage to his life-long friend would not be the hardship he had first thought it might.

A skeleton staff of a single maid, a cook, and a valet arrived in short order, taking his and Caressa's clothing and the trunk of foodstuffs to be stored for use during the week. Kirkland joined Caressa by the fire, rubbing his hands together.

He looked to his companion, tried to think of something to say to the small woman beside him. It seemed so odd, to have nothing to say to a person he had known for so long but about whom he knew very little. When nothing came to mind, Kirkland returned his gaze to the flames dancing in the fireplace.

When he felt a delicate hand settle on his knee, Kirkland felt his heart trip and his cock tighten. Without looking down, he picked up Caressa's hand and lifted it to his lips. He thought of how strong that small hand had felt as she had clutched his back, clawed his skin. Heat flushed Kirkland's cheeks, not with embarrassment but desire. He pressed his lips against the thin skin on the inside of her wrist.

A small whimper erupted from his friend – his wife, and he looked up, seeing Caressa's eyes had glazed over with lust. Before Kirkland could pull her into his arms, someone cleared their throat behind them. Kirkland and Caressa both turned to find the cook smiling at them.

"Would you prefer to rest while I prepare a large meal or would you like something light tonight and retire early?"

Kirkland looked at Caressa from the corner of his eye. "I believe something light will suffice for tonight."

Caressa gasped but she squeezed his hand, conveying her agreement. The little time they had to wait seemed an eternity to Caressa. Wanting nothing more than to be in her husband's arms again, she could do nothing but sit there, fidgeting. Self-doubt began to swirl in her belly, causing her stomach to sour slightly.

She toyed with her bowl of chicken soup, chasing pieces of chicken and vegetables with her spoon. Kirkland ate quickly and voraciously, devouring three bowls in the time it took Caressa to finish her first and only.

Patting her lips dry with her napkin, Caressa hid her mouth when her breath grew short as Kirkland scraped his chair back from the table. His hand appeared before her. "Time to retire, Caressa."

Her hand shook as she laid the stiff linen beside her empty bowl. Setting her trembling fingers in her husband's palm, Caressa allowed Kirkland to pull her to her feet and guide her to a room with a low, wide bed, a roaring fire, a dressing screen and no other furniture.

The maid stood beside the dressing screen and the valet was across the room. Caressa and Kirkland parted, allowing the servants to undress them before leaving the room. Stepping out from behind the screen, Caressa smoothed the lovely rose lace shift over her belly. She looked up to find Kirkland, naked, staring at her, a predatory glint in his eyes.

Kirkland matched her moves as she placed first one then the other knee on the feather mattress. Her shift clutched in her fists, she crawled forward to meet Kirkland in the center of the bed. He reached up and cradled her head in his hands. Kirkland's tongue flicked out and teased her lips.

His fingers traced down her cheeks, the sides of her neck, to rest on her shoulders. He peeled the thin shift from her shoulders, pushed it gently down her arms. His warm, dry palms slid over her breasts, lightly abrading her nipples and eliciting a whimper from Caressa.

The thin cotton of her chemise floated down her waist, past her hips, and pooled at her knees. Kirkland's hands slowly followed its descent. His fingertips grazing the ticklish flesh of her ribs and belly caused Caressa to gasp, swallowing a laugh. When he reached her hips, one hand slid to her front, the other to her back.

Caressa bit Kirkland's lower lip. Her hands grasped his shoulders, her nails digging in to the hard flesh. She needed to hold tightly to something, anything. The large hand at her back slid down to cup one globe of her rear. His other hand petted the hair at the apex of her thighs.

Kirkland's fingers spent what felt like hours just stroking the hair covering her wet mound. Caressa whimpered, begging without words. Kirkland tugged on the crisp hair, causing her to cry out, finally finding her voice. "Please! Touch me, please, 'Land, please!"

She felt her husband smile against her chin. "Of course, Caressa."

Slowly, his fingers moved between her thighs. He pressed against her weeping nether lips, rubbing her, the moisture from her body reducing the nearly painful friction into pleasure. Two fingers slid inside of her. His thumb found that hidden bud that tingled so mercilessly. "Yes! Kirkland!"

Caressa bit into Kirkland's muscled chest, trying hard to stifle her cries. Cruelly, her husband pulled his hand away but quickly jerked her against his body. He kissed her, his lips hard, his tongue forceful as he stroked into her mouth as his body had stroked into hers the night before. Kirkland urged her down to the feathered mattress.

Caressa spread her thighs, inviting her husband between them. He pressed her into the ticking, rubbing his hard sex against her weeping one. Kirkland reached between them and she felt the bulbous head of his sex against her, pushing inside of her.

Still unused to the stretch of her body, Caressa gasped at the small bite of pain but it quickly slid into pleasant pressure as Kirkland slid into her. Caressa moaned and Kirkland pressed his open mouth to hers. He kissed her deeply, his lips crushing hers. As he pulled back, his teeth clamped onto her bottom lip, scraping on the sensitive flesh. Whimpering, Caressa circled her arms around her husband's neck as her legs wrapped around his waist. She pulled him back to her, wanting more of his kisses – cruel and punishing or soft and sweet, it didn't matter to Caressa.

Using her legs, Caressa squeezed her husband closer to her. She squirmed, wriggling her hips, praying silently that he would move. Finally Kirkland pulled away from her, slowly sliding out before dropping his hips, pounding himself into her. Caressa gasped around his tongue and Kirkland's lips left hers.

Kirkland untangled her arms from his neck, sliding his hands to hers and weaving their fingers together. "Tell me you love it. Tell me you love my cock inside of you." His voice was smoky and gritty as she had never heard it before. Caressa nodded her head vigorously but couldn't make herself say the words he wanted to hear.

His hips stopped, his sex deep inside of her. "Tell me, Caressa. I want you say it." Kirkland ground his hips against her. Caressa cried out in pleasure. "Say it."

"Yes!" Caressa cried. "Yes, I love your c-c-cock. I love it inside of me. Please!"

Kirkland slammed his lips onto hers. Caressa thrashed as Kirkland withdrew and returned. He groaned into her mouth, meeting Caressa's whimper. Kirkland pulled his mouth from hers, looked into her eyes, held her gaze as he thrust harder and faster.

Caressa's heels sought for and gained purchase on the bed beneath her. She pressed up as Kirkland ground down and she cried out with every thrust of her husband's hips. It felt as though someone was wrapping ribbons around her waist, silken yet strong, and growing tighter and tighter with every movement of her and Kirkland's bodies. Her eyes slipped shut.

"Caressa."

Without being told, she knew Kirkland wanted her to open her eyes, wanted her to look at him. Blue eyes clashed with green, Caressa couldn't even blink.

Suddenly the ribbons were cut and Caressa screamed the pleasure of her release. She sank her teeth into her bottom lip, her fingernails into the flesh on the back of her husband's hands. Kirkland pumped his hips one more time, groaning her name as he pulsed inside of her.

Kissing her softly one last time, Kirkland pulled away from her, laid beside her and pulled Caressa into his arms. Sleep dragged her eyelids closed as she listened to her husband's slowing heartbeat.

So the days went for their abbreviated wedding trip. Silent days filled with passionate nights. Every time he called her name into the darkness, Caressa hoped she heard more tenderness, heard a little love. She did not know if she was looking for that which wasn't there, but she allowed herself to believe – to hear what she so desperately wanted to hear – if only in those dark hours.

Chapter Nine

Caressa's parent's had returned to welcome Kirkland and Caressa home. Her mother and father had tea with her and told her how empty their home seemed without her shining presence to fill every corner. Caressa laughed as her mother told her stories of her brother's foibles.

"I swear those boys are more excitable without you there, darling. Even our ever-responsible Geoffrey has been misbehaving. Harry convinced him to go into town with him and Geoffrey, uncharacteristically, had a small drink. That hideous little man Bartel was there. He started an argument with your brothers. Harry turned his back on the baron and Bartel hit him with the metal grip on his walking stick."

Caressa's mother shook her head dramatically. "To hear Harry tell it, Geoffrey launched himself at Bartel. Harry insisted it took six men to pull your brother off of the little heathen."

Caressa was truly shocked her subdued brother Geoffrey would do such a thing. "What did Bartel say to start the argument?"

"You brothers will not say. I can only imagine it was horrible. Likely just his ugly venom."

Caressa wasn't convinced. Even full of whiskey, large and solid Harry would not have needed Geoffrey to protect him. And Geoffrey knew that. Whatever Bartel said to her brothers, it was out of the ordinary and far worse than anything they may have already heard from him. Caressa told herself to remember to ask Geoffrey when next she saw him.

Caressa listened as her mother continued to chatter. She was happy for the comfort of the older woman's voice, even if she had little interest in the gossip. She nodded, smiled and laughed when her mother did, but her mind was not on the words her mother was speaking. Her mind was on that night, her husband, and the pleasure he would bring her.

* * *

Caressa pressed her hand against her knee to stop her leg from bouncing. Her nerves ran riot as she waited for the meal to end. She listened to the conversation with less than half an ear, unable to repeat anything said even seconds later. A footman appeared at her elbow, offering to take her half full plate.

Before dessert could be served, Caressa excused herself, begging an aching head. Maisy was in her room waiting for her. "Oh, Miss Caressa, this is a lovely gown." Her maid smoothed the delicate fabric of the night dress Caressa had chosen earlier.

"Isn't it? Hurry, Maisy, I want to be ready by the time my husband comes upstairs."

"Of course, deary." Her maid helped her change her clothing and arrange her hair to fall softly around her shoulders. Maisy left her with a squeeze to Caressa's shoulder. It wasn't long before she heard the main door to the suite open and Kirkland's heavy tread. The only disconcerting thing was he was walking in the wrong direction.

The door across the suite from hers opened and closed. Caressa walked into the sitting room, saw no trace of Kirkland, and so decided she would have to follow him. As she stepped up to the door, she contemplated knocking first but decided against it. Caressa pressed on the lever and opened the door.

Heavy, dark Hepplewhite furniture dominated the room. The deep, masculine colors of the draperies and bed linens seemed to swallow the modest light from the candles and banked fire. Caressa felt as if her small figure was made even more diminutive in the grand scale of the room. She couldn't help but think that Dulcie could walk in here with confidence. Biting her lip, Caressa looked at her husband.

Kirkland was almost naked, his back to her. She let her gaze wander over the sleek muscles that curved into a deep groove along his spine. His smooth rear flexed as he removed one stocking and suspender and then the other.

Unable to resist the call of his gorgeous body, Caressa walked silently to him and laid her hands on his back. His skin was burning hot and she pressed herself closer to that heat. Caressa kissed the smooth skin, brushing her lips across the hard points of his shoulder blades, moving down until she was just above the small of his back. She finally settled her mouth in the valley down the center of his back. Needing to know his taste, the flavor of him on her tongue, Caressa licked up along his backbone.

Kirkland shuddered and turned to face her. His green eyes were bright with passion. He picked her up and placed her on the bed. Before he could lower himself on top of her, Caressa slid from the bed to kneel before him on the floor. She thought of what Dulcie had told her to do. Looking at the size of her husband's cock, Caressa was doubtful she would be able to fit it inside her mouth. But she would try.

Caressa leaned forward and kissed the tip. The skin was smooth and wet. She licked her lips and decided she liked the taste. It was salty and thick. Caressa licked the round cap and Kirkland groaned. She opened her mouth wide and took the top inside. She slid her lips down, but had to retreat when she choked. Wrapping her hand around the root of his cock, Caressa looked at it, trying to decide how she would perform this act.

Kirkland wrapped one hand around hers on his shaft and cupped the back of her head with the other. She looked up into his eyes and he smiled down at her. "Take it slow, love. Just open your mouth and let me do the rest."

Caressa felt her heart flutter at the endearment and did as he asked. Kirkland slipped in past her lips and moved slowly, shallowly, in and out of her mouth. He moved their hands together, stroking the portion of his shaft left untouched by her mouth. He pulled out completely and told her, "Lick along the bottom."

Caressa ran her tongue down his shaft to his sack which he urged her to take into her mouth. She sucked first one small globe then the other into her mouth, the coarse hair tickling her lips. "Run your lips along the sides of my cock, use your tongue."

Caressa pulled away from his sack, pressed her open mouth to the velvety skin of his staff and ran her tongue up to the tip. She sucked the leaking tip once before moving down the opposite side. Caressa swiped the underside of his cock with her tongue, coming back to the cap.

Kirkland reached down and pulled her off of him and to her feet. He turned her away from him and untied the ribbon at her back. The gown sagged and Kirkland caressed the delicate fabric from her shoulders. Caressa's arms hung at her sides and the gown slithered down her body unimpeded.

Kirkland's hands glided around Caressa's slim waist. She shivered, covered his hands with hers. She guided one hand up to cup her breast, and pulled the other down to cover her mound. He didn't press his way inside, instead his fingers rubbed the sensitive skin and crisp hair on the surface. Caressa whimpered and pressed her hips against their hands. She tried pressing his fingers against her, inside her, but he resisted.

"Please, Kirkland."

He rubbed harder. Caressa could just feel Kirkland's fingers against that sensitive nub between her legs. It was frustrating. It built her hunger until she was close to screaming at him.

Dulcie had told her how using words a lady shouldn't enticed Jackson. She had told Caressa what those words were. "Fuck me, Kirkland. I need your cock inside of me. Now. Please!"

Kirkland growled in her ear. "Where did you learn such naughty words, my lovely Caressa?"

"Fuck me," she persisted, ignoring his question.

Kirkland turned her to face him, sat her on the edge of the bed, and pressed her to her back. Standing beside the bed, he raised her legs so that the back of her thighs pressed against his chest. Caressa cried out as he plunged into her.

She watched Kirkland's face. His head tipped back, the cords of his neck stood out in sharp relief. His soft mouth was pressed into a hard line and Caressa saw a muscle tick in his cheek. Kirkland slowly moved his hips, drawing out the pleasure.

Wrapping his arms around her thighs, Kirkland moved his thumbs down and petted the nub of sensation between her legs. Caressa whimpered weakly. She tried to move her hips but Kirkland moved one big, elegant hand and pressed down on her belly, holding her in place.

Along with the pressure came even greater pleasure. Caressa cried, tears rolling across her temples and into her hair. Kirkland moved his hips faster and she begged him to stop. "Please... too much.... Stop...."

Even as she pleaded with him, Caressa reached up and curled her hands around Kirkland's sides, pulling him closer to her, into her. It grew to be too much. Her body spasmed as she reached her breaking point. "Kirkland! Yes, please!"

She scratched at his chest, having lost control of her body. Kirkland tipped his head back. "'Ressa!"

Kirkland fell to his knees, slipping from her so quickly and suddenly, she gasped at the loss. She felt his lips as he kissed the tender skin of her inner thighs. His fingers petted the soft hair covering her sex. One finger glided over the painfully sensitive nub.

Caressa groaned. It felt so good but it was too much. When she tried to push his hand away, Kirkland merely nipped her fingertips and continued to pet her. Her climax came but was not as near to pain as they had in the past. Instead, it lingered until long after Caressa had turned into a boneless mass.

Kirkland rose above her and moved her to the center of his bed. He lay down beside her and pulled her into his arms. She felt his lips and mouth nuzzle her hair and he placed a kiss on her head. Caressa wrapped both hands around his arm and listened as his breathing evened to the deep rhythm of sleep.

Looking into his face, she smiled. A deep warmth filled her chest. She knew that he must have felt something as he touched her tonight. Already, plans for tomorrow night swirled in her mind. She could hardly wait.

Chapter Ten

Caressa looked at the red stain on her shift, cursing her luck. Her woman's time had arrived early. Three weeks of the delicious sensations, of spending night after night in her husband's bed, or he in hers, but naught of it had produced a child. Now, not only did she not want her husband to touch her as she bled, she was not even certain she wanted to see him. She had known something was wrong when she had awoken in a black mood. It was a good thing Kirkland had not been in the bed with her that morning for she did not want him to see her in such a mood, or such a state.

She asked Maisy to bring her breakfast to her bedchamber, not in the mood to join their families for the morning meal. Caressa ate and allowed Maisy to talk her into dressing and joining her parents for the short time they had before they left that day.

She looked at the ring that glittered on her finger. It was a large sapphire surrounded by a dozen small emeralds. Even her dark mood could not stop the smile that came to her lips. Kirkland had told her the jewels reminded her of her eyes. Caressa turned the band this way and that, seeing the colors dance, the gems sparkle.

Maisy cleared her throat, pulling Caressa's attention from her wedding present. "Deary, maybe t'isn't such a bad thing, you bleeding right now. You've spent a lot of time in that young man's bed, but how much time have you spent in his company?"

"As you just pointed out, Maisy, I have spent every night since our wedding night with Kirkland," she replied.

Maisy shook her head, laughing gently. "No, no, Lady Caressa. How much time have you spent talking with him, spending time while not... most pleasantly occupied?"

Caressa shrugged. "We have known each other all our lives. What is left to learn of him?"

"You know him as a friend. It is time to get to know Mr. Perry as your husband and lover." Maisy took hold of Caressa's bejeweled hand and pulled her to her feet.

Caressa felt tears threaten. "He doesn't see me as a wife and barely sees me as a lover. Were I taller with a fuller figure and long red hair, perhaps I could capture his interest. But not this short, too-thin, yellow-haired urchin – I could not turn his head, no matter how hard I tried."

Maisy cupped her cheeks, wiping away the tears that rolled down Caressa's face. Her maid's eyes were kind, sympathetic, and they only served to make her feel more miserable. She sounded so bitter and hateful. And against her own friend! She tried to pull away but her maid would not allow it.

"Lady Dulcie is a fine woman. Beautiful in her own right, true. However, and perhaps it is because I am merely biased as I love you as my own, but she is not nearly as lovely as you. Mr. Perry will come to see this and Lady Dulcie will float from his mind as you consume his thoughts day and night." Maisy smiled and, because Caressa knew she was expecting it, she smiled in return.

Maisy sighed. "That sad excuse for a smile will have to do for now."

Her maid pulled her from the suite and encouraged Caressa down the stairs. Caressa smoothed non-existent wrinkles from the dark blue fabric of her day dress and went to join the family. She found her and Kirkland's mothers in the drawing room. They told her Kirkland was in Konnor's office with him and her father. They were likely discussing Caressa and Kirkland's future and settling the final arrangements of her dowry. She would not see her husband for some time if she knew her father and his penchant to talk business. Caressa sighed in relief.

She was still not ready to face Kirkland. Caressa needed time to regain her good mood and until she did, she didn't want Kirkland to see her. Not listening to the older women, Caressa simply listened to the soothing voices. She closed her eyes and allowed her mind to wander back over her time alone with her husband.

Though they had spoken little while at the cabin, Caressa would always cherish their time there. She would hold close the memories of her husband around her, inside of her, pushing her body towards strange and wonderful sensations with no chance of interruption.

"Do you not agree, Caressa?"

The direct use of her name pulled Caressa out of herself and had her looking to her mother. "I'm sorry, what did you say?"

"Oh, look at her, that dreamy look of love." Kirkland's mother laughed.

Her own mother patted Caressa's knee. "You haven't heard a bit of the conversation, love."

That her mother made it a statement, rather than a question, Caressa was even more embarrassed than she might have been. She felt her cheeks heat and looked at her hands,
wisting in her lap. "No, I haven't. I apologize."

"Oh, it is all right, darling. I well remember when your father and I were wed." She laughed and looked to Kirkland's mother. "We know the feeling well, don't we?"

Kirkland's mother made a non-committal noise and giggled along with Caressa's mother. Forcing a laugh past her lips, Caressa sat up straight, her posture having wilted as she thought of her husband. She pushed her daydreams to the back of her mind and made a concerted effort to listen to her mother and mother-in-law.

The butler came and announced lunch. He informed them they would be eating alone as their husbands were still in her father-in-law's office. The men didn't surface until the women were nearly finished. When the large clock in the main hall sounded off three bells, Caressa's mother and father announced it was time for them to leave. Caressa hugged and kissed her parents goodbye, feeling more bereft than when Kirkland and she had left for their wedding trip. Somehow, this seemed worse. As the door closed behind them, Caressa felt like a small child when she swiped a tear from her cheek.

*   *   *

Kirkland walked into the library and found Caressa curled
onto a settee, a book in her hands, her eyes flying across the pages. He cleared his throat and his wife jumped in her seat, the book

falling to the floor. Her blue eyes flew back and forth from her book to him.

Kirkland walked over to her and picked up the fallen tome. He looked at the cover. George Walker's *The Haunted Castle*. He raised an eyebrow at Caressa and handed her back the volume. A small frown disrupted the smoothness of the skin of her forehead. "I enjoy Mr. Walker's work."

"As do I," said Kirkland as he sat in a leather chair caddy-corner to the chaise his wife occupied. Kirkland reminded himself every day to think of Caressa as his wife, believing it would get easier with time. "All of Mr. Walker's books you will find in this room are mine."

Caressa looked at him with surprise. "Have you read *Theodore Cyphon?*"

Kirkland smiled, "All three volumes."

They spoke for the rest of the afternoon, comparing their favorite authors and tales. Kirkland was delighted to find out that Caressa hated the lighter stories intended for ladies. She enjoyed tales of mystery and suspense, of adventure and danger.

As the setting sun shone through the mullioned windows it painted Caressa's golden hair in pinks and purples. She looked like a fairy and for a moment Kirkland couldn't breathe. His friend was more beautiful than he had ever realized.

It seemed odd that he would notice that here, now. There was nothing remarkable about the moment, nor the setting. They merely sat there talking and he was struck.

Bowers walked into the room just at that moment and announced dinner was ready. Kirkland turned his attention from his wife and thanked Bowers. Later that night, after eating dinner and spending some time with his parents, Kirkland escorted Caressa to their suite.

He knew she would not invite him to her bed this evening, the fact of her condition obvious from her dark dress and the times she would grow quiet and unconsciously rub her belly. Kirkland lifted her hand to his mouth and kissed her knuckles. When Caressa reached up and curled her free hand around the back of his neck, Kirkland wrapped his arms around her waist and pulled her against his chest. He pressed his lips to hers, thrust his tongue into her mouth. The feel of the fingers softly skimming the front of his throat made him gentle the kiss. Slowly, he pulled away and let her go.

"Good night, Caressa."

She smiled shyly at him as she entered her bedchamber. "Good night, Kirkland."

The door closed with a soft click and Kirkland took a moment before he walked across the sitting room and into his own bed chamber. Unwilling for his valet to see his body in its excited state, Kirkland dismissed the man for the evening. He undressed himself slowly, hoping the urgency in his cock would lessen.

It didn't. When he stood bare, even having taken the time to fold the articles of clothing, Kirkland sat on the side of his bed, looking down into his lap. He was painfully erect and wanted to sink himself into Caressa's body. Unfortunately, tonight, that was not an option.

The head of his cock was wet. He slicked the fluid down his shaft. Kirkland lay back on the bed, his legs hanging over the side. One arm thrown over his eyes, Kirkland pictured a woman in his mind. She had long red hair, a generously curved body, and laughing brown eyes.

He had thought of Dulcie before and her image had always help as he calmed his ardor, but now there was something wrong. He shouldn't be thinking of her, another man's wife while he was another woman's husband. But it was more than that, too. It felt wrong.

It was only a fantasy. He was not the first man, he was certain, to think of a woman besides his wife. That didn't make what he was thinking all right. His hand slowed and he shifted the image in his mind. Red turned to gold, the body became slimmer, smaller, and brown turned the color of the sky on a clear, hot summer's day.

Kirkland pumped his hand as he imagined Caressa above him, riding him. His hands on her hips forcing her to his pace. He could almost feel her sharp nails scratching at his chest as she begged him to move faster. Before he could stop it, Kirkland came. He groaned through clenched teeth.

Kirkland lay there for a moment, allowing his breathing and heartbeat to return to normal before getting up to clean himself. The revelation he had made moments ago would have to wait until tomorrow for further examination. He didn't have the energy to think on it now.

*   *   *

The next day Caressa stayed in bed until after luncheon. Her stomach was in knots. Maisy brought her a bladder filled with hot water and she curled into herself around it. After she turned away not only breakfast but lunch as well, Kirkland came to visit her carrying a tray of hot broth and tea.

"Sit up, Caressa."

"No!" She pulled the blankets over her head and snuggled deeper into the mattress. She knew she sounded like a petulant child but she had no interest in food or company. She heard the muffled sound of Kirkland setting down the tray. The blankets disappeared from her head and Kirkland was leaning over her, frowning. "Come now, you must eat."

Caressa rolled over, presenting her back to her husband. She grumbled, "I am not hungry."

Caressa squealed as Kirkland slid his arms around her and lifted her from the bed. He carried her to the dressing table where he had placed the soup and tea and sat on the chair before the small vanity with Caressa in his lap.

She knew the small chair must be uncomfortable for Kirkland. He did not complain, however. Instead he fed her until she finally relented and took the spoon from him. He did not let her leave his lap until she had finished the broth and the tea. When she was done, he pulled her back against his chest and rested his chin atop her head.

"Do you feel better?"

Caressa sighed, plucking at the lacy cuff of Kirkland's sleeve. "Yes, thank you."

They sat quietly for a moment before Kirkland asked, "Is something else wrong?"

Caressa bit her lip, considering telling him everything rolling through her head. She wanted to tell him how she loved him, how it hurt that he loved another – her best friend. She wanted to tell him that she feared he would grow to hate her. Caressa wanted reassurances but was terrified Kirkland would be able to give them.

"No, nothing else," she murmured against his chest.

Kirkland was quiet for so long Caressa knew he didn't believe her. Finally, he sighed and lifted her from his lap, making her stand before him. She thought he would push her to tell him but instead he just stood and looked down into her eyes. He brushed her hair back from her. "All right," he finally murmured and kissed her forehead.

He released her and walked to the door. At the last second he turned back to her. "I expect you downstairs for dinner this evening."

Caressa nodded and Kirkland left the room. She watched the door long after he left the suite. Sometimes Caressa wondered what her future would be like with Kirkland. She wondered if there would be more than friendship and tenderness. Resigning herself to the improbability of more was not only difficult but painful.

*   *   *

That evening at dinner, Caressa tried to eat but her stomach was still too upset. She couldn't eat more than a few bites of the tender lamb on her plate. Tired and feeling ill, she tried to participate in the conversation. Caressa even agreed to sit with Beatrice for a while after the meal.

Kirkland finally took pity on her. After only a short while in the parlor, with his mother, Kirkland entered the room and came to kneel by her chair. He brushed his knuckles down her cheek. "Come along, Caressa. Time to put you to bed."

He took her up to their suite and dismissed Maisy as they entered Caressa's chamber. Kirkland helped her to undress and put her to bed. He sat next to her, his hip brushing hers. Caressa wondered if he would ask to share her bed but he merely brushed back tendrils of hair that had fallen free of the ribbon that held the rest of her locks in a tail at the base of her skull.

Kirkland leaned down and gently kissed her forehead. "Goodnight, love," he whispered.

Caressa's heart stuttered as he uttered the careless endearment. She swallowed around the lump that suddenly blocked her throat. "Goodnight." Her voice rasped and her eyes began to prick with the feeling of oncoming tears. She prayed they wouldn't fall while he was watching and for once her prayers were answered kindly. Kirkland smiled down at her and left the bed, then the room.

Caressa stared up at the ceiling, tears rolling from the corners of her eyes, across her temples, and tickling her scalp as they filtered through her hair. With an upset stomach and an aching heart, she forced herself to find some small respite in sleep. If she couldn't have his love in the waking world, at least she could in her dreams.

Chapter Eleven

Kirkland looked out the study window. For the past two nights, when he had gone to Caressa's bedchamber she had turned him away. While out of bed, she had walked around with a little frown wrinkling the smooth skin between her eyebrows. She barely talked to anyone besides his mother and her maid, Maisy. He knew what was wrong with her naturally, but he was beginning to wonder what was wrong with him.

It was not that he had never gone without a woman's company in his bed. However, it had never bothered him to be alone at night as it did now. He supposed it could be that he had a wife and she should be at his beck and call. That wasn't it.

He just wished she was there at his side for him to hold through the night. If she did not want to share her body with him during this time, he understood but that did not mean she could not sleep in his bed. He missed waking up with her wrapped around him, one slim, soft arm draped across his chest and one leg curled around one of his, her foot snuggled between his calves.

He missed the sensation of her breath fanning his chest. He wanted to press his nose to her silky hair and breathe in the delicious scent of honey that seemed to emanate from her. He needed to feel the soft roundness of her breasts pressed into his side and one pliant globe of her ass in his hand.

Kirkland had always thought Caressa was beautiful but he was beginning to find that she was exceptional. One of the things that had attracted him to Dulcie was her sturdiness. He'd believed she would be best suited to his hard, deep lovemaking. Over the years of admiring her beauty, intelligence and sweetness, he had grown to care very deeply for her. But, if truth be told, it was his perception that she could withstand how he made love to women. Caressa had always struck him as too small, too fragile to respond to him.

Caressa not only responded to his love making but reveled in it. He delighted in the feeling of her clawing at his skin. The way she loved his body with her mouth had shocked him the first time she had fallen to her knees before him. However, he had quickly grown to need that delicious and wanton mouth torturing him. It never seemed to shock or disgust her, what he wanted to do to her body. Tonight, he hoped, he could return to her bed to play.

At breakfast this morning, Kirkland had noticed the frown was gone. She had laughed with his parents over a story his father told. As he left the table, he had bowed to her and Caressa's eyes and smile promised the heat he so enjoyed from her.

Last night's snow had only dusted the landscape, muting the colors but giving everything a sparkling glow. As he looked out over the shimmering trees and hedges, Kirkland wondered why something felt wrong. He had felt guilty after the first few times he had bedded Caressa but the guilt had lessened each time she came to him and begged him so prettily.

Perhaps that was what felt wrong. While he had gone to her bed once or twice, she was the one who reached out to him more often. As he thought of Caressa now, he tried to remember how many conversations they'd had since they married. Too few. They had been friends once and if nothing else, he wanted them to remain friends.

Caressa deserved more, though. She deserved affection, not just physical attention, from him. He *was* fond of her, truly, but perhaps he had not shown her as he should have. Kirkland *knew* he did not show her as he should have.

His decision was made.   Their wedding had been rushed due to a moment of blinding grief and need. He'd had neither the opportunity nor the inclination to court her. It was time he fixed that. Caressa deserved to be wooed, and he would begin tonight.

Chapter Twelve

After dinner that evening, Kirkland asked Caressa to join him for a sleigh ride. The idea of traveling the powder dusted countryside with Kirkland overrode the desire to stay inside where it was warm. She wrapped a thick wool scarf around her neck, tugged on kid leather gloves, and pulled a heavy, fur-lined cloak around her shoulders.

Meeting Kirkland on the front steps, Caressa smiled up into his emerald gaze. Kirkland returned her smile, taking her hand and carefully escorted her to the sleigh as the driver pulled the horses to a stop. Once she and Kirkland were settled in the back of the sleigh with a heavy blanket covering their laps, a maid came out of the house carrying two cloth wrapped bundles. Kirkland took one from the girl and bent over Caressa to raise her feet and place the heated brick under them.

He took the other brick and placed it under his own feet before telling the driver that they were ready. The horses jerked to life, pulling away from the house and into the night.

The moonlight reflecting off the snow made it possible to see the scenery they passed. The icy wind bit into Caressa's cheeks, nose, and forehead but she didn't care. The heat from Kirkland's body and the warmed brick kept the rest of her comfortable.

She looked out at the trees to the right of their transport. A family of deer stood at the wood line, their noses digging through the snow to get to the grass beneath it. They hit a small bump, which jostled Caressa, startling her and making her yelp. Kirkland reached out for her, pulling her back until she was nestled in his side, his arm wrapped tightly around her shoulders.

Caressa buried her nose in the wool of his winter coat, breathing deep the faint scent of him that underlined the smell of the wool. She tipped her head back, looking into the sky and gasped.

"What?"

Caressa pointed to the stars. "Look at that!"

Kirkland looked up and hummed when he saw the shooting stars flying across the sky. Caressa was enthralled with the display of flashing lights. Kirkland nuzzled the hood of her cape away from her ear and the sensation of his hot breath swirling into the sensitive shell made her shiver. "Make a wish."

Caressa watched and wished on the next star to rocket across the inky expanse. *Please,* she called out from her heart. *Please, let him love me.*

She closed her eyes, praying for the wish to come true. She felt Kirkland's warm lips press against her forehead. "What did you wish for, Caressa?"

Looking up into his eyes, she couldn't say the words aloud. Thankfully, the rules of wishes wouldn't allow her to tell. "If I want my wish to come true, I cannot tell you."

Kirkland chuckled and sat back, cuddling Caressa into his side. They continued around the estate. Caressa saw more animals, most staying close to the tree line, others bravely dashing across the snow covered fields. Three foxes, likely a vixen and her kits, ran alongside the sleigh, their small but lean bodies matching pace with the horses. They veered off suddenly and Caressa supposed they caught the scent of a meal.

When she was younger, Caressa had wondered what it was like to run wild. To be free of the confines of society. To not have to be perfect. Those foxes could change their direction between one heartbeat and the next. They had no need to worry over their hair, their clothing, their posture, their stations in life.

But now, as an adult, Caressa no longer had to wonder. She sat beside the answer. His arm was curled around her, telling her why she had fretted and worked so hard to become the perfect lady. She'd had only one desire since she had met him – to be his wife, his love.

She could only hope that over time his feelings for her would grow. She knew he cared for her. She knew he lusted for her.

Caressa hoped those two would coalesce in Kirkland's heart to create what she felt every time she thought of him, looked at him, kissed and held him.

She also knew her hopes were the romantic dreams of a child. More marriages than not contained no love. They were partnerships created by two families, or by His Majesty, to better benefit the families or the king's intentions. She knew many of her married friends had lovers and their husbands, mistresses. She did not want that existence for herself and Kirkland. For the children they might someday have.

She felt the horses slow to a stop. Looking around, Caressa saw they had returned to the house. She had been so engrossed in her own thoughts, she hadn't realized they had turned around and made the return journey.

Kirkland stepped down from the sleigh then turned back to lift Caressa out of the transport. They made their way into the manor house and up to their suite. At her bedroom door, Kirkland whispered, "Goodnight."

He pressed a soft, chaste kiss to her lips before retreating to his bedchamber for the night. Caressa felt like she was walking on clouds. She also felt terribly bereft that her husband wasn't spending the night in her bed. Her monthly had gone and though she would have welcomed him, she was happy to wait a day before lying with him again.

*   *   *

Caressa sat in Beatrice's solar. Her mother-in-law was sitting across from her, a small set of hoops and piece of linen in her hands. She had asked Caressa several times what she thought of the roses she was embroidering onto the piece of cloth. Caressa indulged Lady Perry, telling her they were beautiful. She did not tell the woman the small butterfly she had stitched perching on the edge was a frightening looking mass of black and red thread.

Caressa bent over her own rings, larger than those her mother-in-law was using. The embroidery pattern she was creating was a large oak tree. Its bare branches covered in snow as well as snow covering the ground. The backdrop was going to show more trees, less defined than the oak, and the night sky. There would be a bright star flying across the top. She was stitching a memory of her and Kirkland's sleigh ride.

Her stomach suddenly clenched, reminding Caressa of how nauseous she had felt that morning. She had eaten very little at breakfast. It was odd. While she had felt sick during her monthly, that was not unusual. It was, however, unusual for the feeling to continue afterward.

When Bowers entered the room to inform them that luncheon was served, Caressa followed Kirkland's mother from the room but wasn't truly happy to eat. She picked at the food on her plate but as she filled her stomach little by little, she began to feel better.

"Caressa?"

Looking across the table at Kirkland, she saw that he was staring at her. She looked around and found both of his parents with the same surprised look on their faces. She spied her plate, noticing for the first time that it was almost completely empty while theirs were still filled. A hot blush scorched her face.

"Sorry. I must have been hungrier than I realized." Caressa kept her head down and refused additional portions, finishing what was left as slowly as possible.

Dinner that evening was much the same, only this time Caressa did not beg off from extra portions. She ate her meal three times over, feeling slightly bloated but satisfied when she could finally eat no more.

"That's quite the appetite you have, my dear," Lord Perry said after everyone was finished.

Caressa blushed but giggled as she did so. Everyone laughed with her and they retired to the lounge where Kirkland challenged her to a game of chess. Being raised to be a proper lady, Caressa let him beat her three times. She knew he had realized she let him win when he began positioning his pieces in easily beaten configurations. Caressa refused the bait.

"I know you're better than that, Caressa." Kirkland removed his dinner jacket and hung it off one of the wings of the chair he occupied.

"I don't know what you mean, Kirkland," she answered guilelessly.

He growled low enough so that only she might hear. "If you do not play with the skill I know you have, we will not leave this table."

She could see the playfully challenging gleam in his eyes and smiled at him. Caressa won the next four games until Kirkland conceded. Though she could tell her husband was close to shooting himself in the foot for goading her into really playing, but he had a smile on his face, letting her know he had enjoyed the contest.

Again that night, Kirkland left her at her door with a sweet kiss. After eating so much at dinner, she was grateful he did not want to bed her. She yawned, her mouth stretching so wide the corners of her mouth stung. She prayed as Maisy undressed her and she slipped into her nightrail. Caressa prayed that tomorrow night her husband would come to her bed, or entice her into his.

Once in bed, with sleep forcing her eyes to close, she dreamt of all the delicious things she wanted to do to Kirkland the next night.

Chapter Thirteen

As she helped Caressa dress for dinner, Maisy flitted around, a small smile on her face. She avoided making eye contact with Caressa. Knowing her maid was hiding something, Caressa finally asked, "What are you not telling me, Maisy?"

Her maid stopped, looking at Caressa with large innocent eyes. "I don't know what you're talking about, deary." The maids removing the tub Caressa had used to bathe giggled. Maisy shot them a scowl before turning her attention back to Caressa.

Caressa opened her mouth to insist Maisy tell her the secret she was keeping, but the maid cut her off. "Now, now, Miss Caressa, it's time for dinner. Run along."

Caressa frowned as her maid pulled her from her seat and nudged her to the door of her bedchamber. As she stepped out into the suite's sitting room, she saw what could only have been Maisy's secret. All of the furniture had been moved to the perimeter of the room and a small round table had been placed in the center. Kirkland stood next to the table dressed in dark blue dinner attire with a bright white shirt and cravat.

"Good evening, Caressa."

"Good evening, Kirkland." She watched as footmen entered the suite carrying serving trays. They deposited their items on the low table that would normally sit in the center of the furniture configuration and left the room. Maisy nudged her again, this time in the direction of her husband. Caressa looked back and scowled at her maid. Maisy only smiled at her, her eyes sparkling as she closed the door between Caressa and herself.

Kirkland pulled out one of the small chairs and waited while she walked forward and sat down. He rounded the table and took his own seat. The warm smile he sent her made Caressa's heart race faster, made her breath catch. Kirkland's eyes trailed down to her upper chest, left exposed by the scooped neckline of her dress.

Caressa felt the tips harden and watched as her husband's eyes darkened. Kirkland looked into her eyes once again and his smile went from warm to deliciously wicked. He turned from her and lifted the domes off of the servers and prepared a plate for Caressa then one for himself.

They ate in silence. Caressa had no idea what to say to Kirkland and he seemed perfectly content merely to watch her. Caressa toyed with the fragrant lamb on her plate. She watched Kirkland through her lashes, waiting for him to say something, anything.

Caressa took a bite and nearly choked when she felt Kirkland's foot rub against the inside of her ankle. The table hid his movement from view. She hadn't even seen him move an inch. She looked directly at him. Kirkland simply smiled at Caressa and continued eating.

When the meal was finished, Kirkland sat back in his chair and eyed Caressa so long she began to fidget. She brushed her fingers over her bodice and hair, trying to dust and smooth anything out of place. When he continued to just look at her, Caressa felt her cheeks heat and felt her chin take on a stubborn angle. "What?" She asked, exasperated by her husband's silence.

Kirkland's smile, the same wicked one he had worn all through dinner, grew wider. "I was just thinking of how lovely you look tonight. Thinking of how much lovelier you would be in my bed."

Caressa felt wetness grow between her thighs. Kirkland rose from his chair and held out his hand. Caressa slipped her fingers into his palm and rose to her feet. Kirkland walked her slowly into his bed chamber, to his bed, and turned to face her. He kissed her softly, undressed her slowly. Caressa shivered. The feel of Kirkland's fingers fluttering over her skin made her hungry, *starving*, for more.

When she felt his fingertips graze her nipples, Caressa stepped closer to Kirkland. His hands became trapped between them, his palms pressed against her breasts. Kirkland growled into her mouth and squeezed the small mounds, her nipples pinched between his fingers. Caressa whimpered. She curled her arms around his neck, pressing as close to him as she could.

Kirkland pulled his hands free, causing Caressa to cry out with loss. His long fingers, his strong hands, smoothed down her back, over her rear. He broke the kiss, trailing his lips down her cheek, her jaw, her neck. When his hands reached the backs of her thighs, his fingers curled around her legs. Lifting her, Kirkland pulled her knees up to his waist, turned, and tipped Caressa back onto the bed.

He nipped her lips with his teeth as he pulled away to stand up between her legs. Kirkland removed his waist coat and unbuttoned the vest beneath as well as the buttons at his wrists. He folded his sleeves up his arms until they banded above his elbows, exposing his tanned, muscular forearms. Removing his cravat took ages. When he finally threw the cloth aside, Caressa reached for the closure of his trousers but Kirkland stepped back before kneeling on the floor.

Kirkland's large hands swept up her legs, starting at Caressa's toes and smoothing slowly, sensually up until his fingers formed a triangle around her curls. Caressa vibrated with anticipation, waiting breathlessly for Kirkland to enter her. She jumped when she felt his tongue lick firmly up the crease of her sex. She gasped when she felt his fingers pull her open and the tip of his tongue lash lightly at the wonderfully sensitive nub.

"Kirkland," she moaned. "More. Please."

Caressa thrashed her hips, trying desperately to make him press his tongue harder, flick his tongue faster. Kirkland refused. He pinned her hips to the bed, continuing the frustratingly light strokes. Unable to tolerate any more teasing, Caressa reached down. She wound her fingers through his hair, dug her nails into his scalp.

Kirkland growled deep in his throat. She felt his lips circle the nub he was teasing. His tongue circled, hard and fast. Kirkland sucked on the nub like he would one of her nipples, making it throb, making the blood pound in that low, intimate region.

Caressa felt that wonderful tightening in her belly. Her body began to shake. Bringing her feet up onto the mattress, Caressa pushed her hips up to grind her sex against Kirkland's mouth. Sobbing as the tightness snapped, releasing energy in an explosion. Light danced behind her eyelids. Her belly convulsed.

Caressa bit her lip, forcing back words of love she could never give her husband. Kirkland kissed his way up her body causing her to shiver. He slipped an arm around her waist, moving her into the center of the bed. Kirkland collapsed beside her.

When Caressa finally caught her breath, she looked up into Kirkland's face. His eyes were closed, his mouth lax, and the movement of his chest was subsiding into the easy rhythm of sleep. With the hand caught between her body and his, Caressa hesitantly reached for Kirkland's shaft. She found it limp and wet. It seemed her husband had found pleasure in pleasuring her.

Smiling to herself, Caressa closed her eyes and drifted off to sleep.

*   *   *

Kirkland awoke to the feel of Caressa's hand curled around his cock. He groaned softly into his pillow. He grew hard and pumped his hips.   Her hand moved with him, frustrating him
with the lack of friction.

Never having felt this lack of control, Kirkland rolled atop Caressa and kissed her awake. As she began to respond to his lips, tongue, and teeth, he pushed his way into her body. Caressa cried out, her legs curling around his hips.

The hot, tight, slick grip of her body had Kirkland's head spinning. He thrust in and out, hard and slow, savoring the feel of her body sucking him back into her. He wove his fingers through hers, pressing them into the pillow her head thrashed upon.

"Yes, yes, faster Kirkland, please!" The sound of her words, begging for more, shot heat down his spine, forcing his hips to pick up speed. Kirkland slammed his hips against her, ground and twisted his lower belly, working to abrade her clit before pulling away.

Caressa's body began to spasm around his cock. He slowed his pace, loving the way she moaned in distress as he took her away from the edge of her orgasm. Kirkland relished the bite of her sharp fingernails into the flesh on the back of his hands. She tried to thrust against him but Kirkland pinned Caressa's hips with his own.

"Please Kirkland, don't stop! Please move!"

Kirkland nuzzled aside the damp golden strands at Caressa's temple. "You love it when I make you wait. You love
feeling desperate for me."

"You're cruel. I don't love it. I hate it. I hate it! Please!" She tossed her head violently.

"Not until you admit it." Kirkland twisted his hips, swirling his cock inside Caressa, grinding against her clit.

Sobbing, Caressa nodded her head violently. "Yes! Yes! I love it! Everything you do to me – everything!"

Kirkland began thrusting again, fucking so hard into her body he had to release her hands and wrap his arms around her to prevent her from banging her head on the solid wood head board. Caressa screamed, her nails scratching at his back, her body contracting and releasing his cock as she came so hard even Kirkland saw stars.

"Kirkland!" She screamed in his ear, practically deafening him.

"Caressa!" He cried out as he poured himself into her body. How had he gone so many days without bringing her to his bed? How had he gone so long without this sweet bliss he'd only ever reached with the woman in his arms?

Kirkland kissed her ear, her collarbone, her throat. He nipped the point of Caressa's chin. Her soft lips were parted as she gasped for breath and Kirkland swooped down, gently thrusting his tongue into her mouth. Her hands smoothed down his back, as if apologizing for scoring his flesh.

He wanted to tell her she had no need to apologize. Kirkland wanted Caressa to understand that he loved it when she lost control, but he could barely find the strength to roll from atop her, let alone speak those words. Kirkland pulled her close, tucking the crown of Caressa's blond head beneath his chin, before closing his eyes and falling into an exhausted but sated sleep.

Chapter Fourteen

The smell of the breakfast foods had Caressa's stomach churning. She took a small bite of egg and ate a piece of dry toast before deciding eating was not for her that morning. In no mood to do any of the normal activities, she sat in the library and read.

Kirkland found her before setting out with his father to London. "I will return in just a few days, sweet. Is there anything you would like me to bring back with me?"

The endearment spread a warm feeling through her chest but she ignored it and concentrated on his question. Thinking of the chocolates her papa would buy her from a candy maker on High Street, Caressa shook her head. She would love some chocolates but with the sourness in her stomach of late, she didn't dare ask for them. "I cannot think of anything," she fibbed. "Just come back to me as soon as you can."

Kirkland kissed the top of her head then nuzzled her crown with his nose. "In a few days, then."

Caressa nodded after he pulled away and smiled brightly at him when he turned at the door for a last look. Only letting her smile fall after she heard the horses pull away, Caressa rubbed her belly. The nausea had subsided since breakfast but she was still in no mood to eat. Neither was she in the mood to stay there with only Beatrice for company. She was a lovely woman but Caressa could not take another day of being cooped up with Lady Perry.

She considered going to see her family but decided against it. Her mother and father would be livid at her should she arrive at their estate in Courtney with the roads in their current state. Torningate, however, was a possibility. She missed her best friend and wanted to see how Dulcie and Jackson were getting on.

Caressa called for Bowers and asked him to ready a transport so that she might go and visit Torningate. Bowers tried to talk her out of going. "If I may say, ma'am, the roads are very bad. If anything were to happen to you, Young Master Perry would never forgive me."

Caressa doubted that but said aloud, "It will be all right, Bowers. Nothing will happen to me or to the sleigh. Please, have it ready in half an hour."

Bowers hesitated before bowing. "Yes, ma'am."

Half an hour later, Caressa and Maisy were bundled into the sleigh with heavy blankets and heated bricks. The journey to Torningate took a few hours longer than it should have but they made it to Jackson and Dulcie's estate not long after nightfall. Dulcie had a look of delighted surprise on her face as she hugged Caressa.

"I hadn't expected to see you so soon! What brings you here in such dreadful conditions?" She pulled Caressa into the dining room where Jackson waited for them. He came toward the pair, smiling in welcome. "Hello, Caressa."

Accepting a kiss on the cheek from her old friend, Caressa shrugged out of the heavy cloak she wore, allowing the butler to take it away. "Hello Jackson. I'm sorry to arrive unannounced. Kirkland and Konnor went to town for business and I was left all alone with the Baroness. It is nothing against Beatrice, Kirkland's mother is a wonderful woman, but I needed to get out of the house."

"Don't be ridiculous!" Dulcie exclaimed. "You are always welcome."

They all sat down and waited as the food was brought to the table. The conversation was light with Dulcie recounting gossip her mother sent in her last letter. "Ah, but you know Mother. She doesn't truly believe anything until it has been confirmed by the parties involved. She is, however, all too happy to believe what she heard about Bartel."

Jackson cleared his throat, shaking his head when Dulcie looked at him. In a loud whisper that made her husband chuckle, Caressa's friend said, "I will tell you later."

After they were finished eating, Dulcie accompanied Caressa to her chamber. Once ensconced in the guest suite, Dulcie started to laugh evilly. Maisy helped Caressa undress and prepare for bed.

"Well?" Caressa prompted.

Clicking her tongue in a disgusted manner, Dulcie told her what her mother's letter said of the horrid man that Dulcie had at one time been betrothed to. "He was found with Lt. General Griffon's son, in a very compromising position."

"Dulcie, you found him in the center of an orgy!" Caressa reminded her friend.

"Yes, but he wasn't made to marry my spinster aunt. The Lt. General has a twin sister, never married, who has agreed to make Bartel's life hell! According to mother's letter, the sister will be bringing several staff members with her. If Bartel is ever found to be unfaithful to the Lt. General's sister, Griffin will call him out and Griffin is a massively better shot and a tremendously better swordsman than my dear ex-betrothed."

"I do feel rather bad for his soon-to-be-wife. I've met her. She's a lovely woman, in her way. Very humorous. Oh well, I think she is as disgusted with Bartel *infecting,* as she put it, her nephew as the Lt. General is." Dulcie shrugged.

Caressa laughed softly. Bartel deserved his *good fortune.* She thanked Maisy for her assistance, dismissing her for the night. Sitting beside Dulcie, Caressa asked about the suddenly thoughtful expression on her face.

"I feel rather bad for the Griffin boy. He's a very nice young man. Just another life damaged by that horrible man, Bartel. Cares more about his own pleasures than those hurt by them." Dulcie shook her head.

She shook her head before turning a bright smile on Caressa. Her friend pulled her into a hug before leaving her seat on the bed and walking to the door. "I'm so glad you came for a visit, Caressa. Have a good night."

After Dulcie left, Caressa climbed under the covers. Tossing and turning, her mind ran through that night months ago. Her best friend, the arms of the man Caressa loved wrapped around Dulcie. She had thought of that night many times. Her heart still broke at the vision.

Caressa fell into a restless sleep, the sight of Kirkland's lips touching Dulcie's foremost in her mind.

The next morning, as she sat with Dulcie and Jackson, Caressa fidgeted with her food, not eating much. The aromas made her stomach turn even though it smelled delicious.

Spending the day with Dulcie was harder than she had imagined it would be. Every time Dulcie laughed, the sound grated on her nerves. Every time Dulcie smiled, Caressa wished her teeth would fall from her head. Every time Dulcie touched her, Caressa wanted to slap her hand away, slap her face. She wanted to rage at Dulcie.

Before they separated to ready for dinner, Dulcie took her hands and sat with her on the chaise lounge in the guest room.

"Caressa, I've gotten the impression that something is wrong. You've barely eaten all day. I've seen more than one grimace on your face. You've barely laughed at all. What's wrong?" Feeling the tears roll down her cheeks, Caressa snatched her hands from Dulcie's grip.

"What's wrong? What's *wrong*? As if you did not know!" Caressa broke. She couldn't hold in her emotion anymore. Getting up to pace the floor in front of the chaise, she shouted at the woman who had been her best friend since they were babes. "How do you think it feels, Dulcie, living with a husband, loving a man, who is in love with someone else?"

A look of horror came over Dulcie's face. Her hands covered her mouth. "No... Caressa..."

"No! Don't! I saw you! I saw you kissing Kirkland. How could you?"

Shaking her head, Dulcie rose and took Caressa by the shoulders. "No, Caressa, I didn't kiss him."

"You did! You kissed Kirkland! He kissed you! He denied me on our wedding night because of you!" A sob tore from her throat. "I will never hear him say the words *I love you* because he doesn't love me. He loves you, Dulcie! I will never hold his heart because you have it in your hands, and you don't even care!"

The door to the attached servant's quarter opened, a wide-eyed Maisy poking her head into the room. "Maisy, pack our bags. We're leaving tonight. Right now."

Dulcie wrung her hands. "Caressa, please, listen to me. I never wanted to hurt you. Please, Caressa, please believe me."

Caressa angrily swiped the tears from her face. "I can't bear to look at you. I can't bear to listen to your voice or be in your company a moment longer."

Maisy had everything prepared in mere minutes. Caressa led the way down the stairs and to the front door. She pulled on her cloak, pulled up the hood, and walked out the front door without another word. There she waited until her driver pulled the sleigh to a stop in front of her.

Caressa and her maid got settled into the sleigh. She didn't look back to the house until they pulled away. In the doorway, Dulcie was wrapped in Jackson's arms, her body heaving as though with sobs.

"Oh, deary."

Caressa looked to her maid. Her own tears began anew. Sobs wracked her body. As she laid her head in the older woman's lap and cried, she wondered if she could ever find it in her heart to forgive her friend. And if Dulcie could ever forgive her.

Chapter Fifteen

Kirkland looked at the sapphire necklace he had bought for Caressa during his trip to London. He hoped she liked it. The minute he had laid eyes on the elongated oval sapphire with three small yellow diamonds on the bottom, three on each side, and three yellow diamonds set in the bale, he had known it would be perfect for his wife.

He laughed to himself. Thinking of Caressa as his wife was coming easier and easier. He enjoyed her body and he enjoyed her mind. He could not wait to arrive at Lynnwood Hall. He wanted to be alone with Caressa – and not only to give her his gift.

* * *

The pain started shortly after she left Torningate. All the way home, her stomach spasmed over and over. Maisy made the driver pull over when they crossed an inn. She asked the innkeeper for broth and a hot stone for her lady.

Her maid had to force the broth down Caressa's throat as she would not voluntarily swallow the clear soup. They left after the driver paid for their service and the innkeeper passed a flannel hot stone up to Maisy. Her maid held Caressa in her lap, the stone pressed to her belly.

Now she lay in her bed, asking, begging for Kirkland. He had still not returned home from London. Caressa wrapped her arms around her middle, moaning as the muscles cramped yet again. She had already been sick several times since arriving back at Lynwood and now she suffered dry heaves as her stomach had nothing else to give up to the chamber pot.

Maisy brought another bladder filled with hot water. They were doing nothing to ease the rhythmic clench and release of her abdominal muscles. When her maid tried to make her eat, the clenching worsened at the smell of the food.

She heard rushed, heavy footsteps coming down the hall, into her and Kirkland's suite.

"Caressa?" She pried open her eyes at the feel of fingertips on her cheek. He was here. He was finally home.

Kirkland called out, told Maisy to send someone for the family doctor. Her heart would have warmed at the concern in his eyes, had her stomach not turned and sent more unproductive heaves to wrack her body.

"It's all right, 'Ressa. Everything is going to be all right." Kirkland kissed her forehead. He left her but only for a few moments as he removed his jacket, boots, and cravat so that he could join her on the bed.

Kirkland wrapped his arms around her. He didn't leave her side until late the next day when the doctor arrived. Even then, his father and several of the male members of the household staff had to pull him from the bedchamber.

He paced across the common room of the suite. When the doctor left Caressa's bedroom he had a slight smile on his face. Kirkland crossed to the man. "Well?"

"Oh, I would say she's well enough." The doctor laughed but quickly choked off the sound when he saw the look on Kirkland's face. "Ahem, um, yes. Lady Caressa is fine. The only real problem is that she is not eating enough. She should be eating for two and she is barely taking in enough for herself."

Kirkland felt light-headed for a moment. "Eating for two," he whispered. "Are you saying my wife is with child?"

The doctor nodded and clapped Kirkland on the shoulder, giving him a nervous smile. "That's right, son. I would say in a few months I will be introducing you to your heir or a delightful princess all your own."

Kirkland needed to sit down. Caressa was pregnant. Scrubbing a hand over his face, Kirkland took several deep breaths. That was it then. If they had a son, there was no reason to continue sharing Caressa's bed. A shaft of cold shot through his chest but Kirkland dismissed it. He had told himself that once Caressa had given him an heir, he would no longer force himself on her.

The night before he left for London came to mind. When he made her admit that she loved what he did to her. When he had come so hard his heart had stopped. When it had only begun beating again when he had looked into her eyes. Kirkland pushed the memory from his mind. He couldn't think of those moments. Not now. Maybe never again.

*   *   *

Through the sleepy haze of laudanum, Caressa watched Kirkland enter the room and approach the bed. The pain and retching had finally stopped but the doctor did not leave the laudanum behind, for which she was very grateful. A blurry Kirkland sat on the edge of the bed, looking down at her.

He lifted his hand and rested it gently on her belly. The feeling of his hand, rubbing in gentle circles, made Caressa sigh. "I cannot believe we are having a child."

Caressa placed her hand over his. "Isn't it wonderful?"

Kirkland's eyes flew to hers and he removed his hand from her stomach. "Yes, wonderful." He rose from the bed walked over to one of the large windows showing a cloudy sky. Absently, Caressa wondered if it would snow. Kirkland's voice breaking the silence startled her in her addled state. "The doctor told me your sickness should be over soon. He said it usually only lasts a few weeks early on in pregnancy, though some women will be ill every day until the child is born."

Her husband turned toward her, walking back to the bed to lean over her, his hands on either side of her head, his face directly over hers. "He also said you must eat. Whether you feel like it or not. Whether you feel sick or not. You must eat, not only for your sake, but the child's, as well. Understand?"

Caressa raised her hand, using her fingertips to gently trace his dark brows. "I understand, Kirkland."

He closed his eyes and turned his face into her caress. He pressed his lips to the sensitive skin of her wrist, placing a gentle kiss there before pulling away and walking to the door.

Caressa frowned. "Kirkland? Won't you stay tonight?"

"Yes, Caressa. I am merely going to see the doctor to the door. I will return momentarily." With that he left the room.

Caressa forced herself to stay awake until her husband returned. He was wearing a heavy robe of quilted green silk. Approaching the bed, Kirkland reached into the pocket and removed a long black box. Caressa took it when her husband presented it to her.

"My beautiful, wonderful wife. Thank you for giving me this perfect gift. Mine does not begin to touch the magnitude of yours, but I hope it conveys my esteem of you."

Smiling, Caressa opened the box and gasped at the necklace inside. The sapphire and diamonds sparkled in the flickering light of the candle that sat on her bedside table. Kirkland lifted the necklace from the box and placed it so the pendant rested on the exposed skin of her chest. Caressa sighed when her husband then kissed above, below, and to either side of the large stone. "Your beauty vastly outshines that of my gift, but it would not matter what I gave you."

"Thank you, Kirkland."

Her husband smiled down at her, caressing her cheek before rising and removing his robe. He wore a long sleeping shirt beneath and didn't remove it when he returned to the bed. Slipping in beside her, Kirkland pulled Caressa into his arms.

Caressa smiled, turning into his embrace and allowing her eyes to close. Finally allowing the laudanum to take her under, her drug induced sleep was deep and dreamless.

Chapter Sixteen

The next morning, Caressa forced down a large breakfast. Her stomach protested but she refused to get sick. Her baby needed nourishment. Looking down at her belly, Caressa placed her hands over the flat surface. She could not believe she was having a baby. She and Kirkland had created a tiny being.

Caressa raised her head when Kirkland covered her hands with one of his. He had a gentle smile on his handsome face. "Have you had enough to eat?"

Caressa nodded, smiling at her husband. Kirkland escorted her back to her bedchamber, promising to be back when the midday meal was ready and they would take a short walk outside before allowing her to rest before dinner. Caressa insisted she wasn't so fragile that she had to remain in bed until the child was born. Kirkland argued that the doctor had insisted she was.

Huffing her irritation, Caressa asked, "Did he truly order me to stay in bed the majority of the day?"

Kirkland curled one arm around her waist and the hand of the other wrapped around her upper arm. He helped her climb up the stairs as if she were newly blind or completely soused. "If you hadn't worked so hard to make yourself ill to begin with, he wouldn't have felt compelled to order bed rest. Until you rebuild your strength you will see more of your bedchamber than any other room."

"I didn't make myself sick, I'm having a child," Caressa said irritably.

When they reached the top of the stairs, Kirkland turned her to face him. He took her face in his hands and stared deeply into her eyes. "Women in your condition are supposed to grow plump. If anything, you are thinner than the day we were wed. Your bones are more prominent. I hadn't realized before last night and I feel a hundred times the fool for allowing you to do such a thing to yourself. From now on you will eat full meals and rest."

Caressa felt her cheeks grow hot with the gentle reprimand. "There is no need to speak to me as if I am a child," she mumbled.

Kirkland pressed his lips to her forehead before steering her to their suite and her chamber. "I will return when lunch is ready. Don't forget to dress in something warm."

Caressa nodded and watched her husband disappear. Maisy entered and helped her strip down to her chemise then lifted the blankets and waited until Caressa crawled onto the bed. She felt like she was a child again only now Maisy handed her a book rather than sitting down to read to her.

The morning passed too slowly. Caressa finished one book and asked Maisy to get her another. When footsteps sounded outside of her door, Caressa found Kirkland there, book in hand, rather than her maid. Caressa smiled and her husband smiled back.

There was something in his smile, in the expression encompassing his handsome face. He looked... sad, resigned. "Is something wrong?"

Kirkland jumped a little, as though he was surprised by her question. He quickly shook his head, his smile widening. "No, no. What could be wrong, hmm? My beautiful wife is having my child. No, Caressa, nothing is wrong." He walked to the side of the bed, gently laying the book he held on the small table beside the bed. "Luncheon will be served shortly. Maisy will be up in a moment, then we will go downstairs."

Kirkland looked at her for a moment, that same strange expression on his face, before leaning over to kiss her on the forehead. He left the room, her maid appearing only seconds after he disappeared from sight. Her maid tsked. "That handsome, insane man of yours told me to dress you warmly, that you're going out after you eat. It is bitterly cold outside! It snowed again last night. Insane man...."

Nonetheless, Maisy dressed her in a green wool dress, thick and warm. Kirkland reappeared and escorted her down to the dining room. After eating more than she normally would, under the watchful eyes of her husband and his family, he bundled her into her fur-lined cloak. Bowers opened the door and bowed to them as they passed.

A nearly pristine layer of bright white, broken only by a trail that wound its way along the front of the house and disappeared at either corner, covered the world with a delicate and cold beauty. The path was bordered by small mounded peaks of snow, all of it so fresh that it told Caressa the trail was cleared only today. They kept the pace slow. The cold nipped at her cheeks and the tip of her nose, but Caressa gladly suffered the small discomforts in favor of spending the quiet time alone with Kirkland.

They said nothing as they walked. Kirkland kept her hand tucked in the crook of his elbow, his hand over hers, holding tightly. By the time they had circled the house and were ready to go back inside, Caressa's nose was numb but she was smiling, happy. Kirkland insisted she return to bed until dinner.

Dinner was another large meal. Caressa was not feeling well but forced herself to eat until smiles creased the faces of her fellow diners. Beatrice cleared her throat. "We were thinking of having a celebration in honor of you and Kirkland having a child, Caressa. We will, of course, wait until the snow melts but I wanted to know how you felt about having a party."

Caressa smiled broadly. "That sounds wonderful!"

Caressa looked to Kirkland who smiled indulgently at her and his mother. "Whatever you would like, Caressa," he said, patting her hand.

For the rest of the evening, until Kirkland insisted she return to bed, Caressa and her mother-in-law planned and plotted the celebration. When Caressa tried to hide a yawn behind her hand, Kirkland chuckled and insisted she come with him to go back to bed.

Kirkland joined her in her bed, again dressed in a long sleeping shirt. His arms wrapped around her and she snuggled into his chest. As her eyes began to droop, she thought of how happy she was, in the arms of the man she loved with his child safely under her heart.

* * *

Kirkland woke hard as stone and his wife kissing her way down his chest. His nightshirt was pushed up to his shoulders and Caressa's lips were wrapped around one of his nipples, sucking hard and grazing the very tip with her teeth. Her slim, cool hands were running up and down his sides, every downward stroke bringing her hands closer and closer to his throbbing erection.

He groaned and her mouth came away from his skin. Looking down at him, Caressa smiled and moved her hips down from his belly until her soft rear rubbed against his aching cock. Caressa's hands left his skin tingling as she pulled them away to drag the skirt of her shift slowly up her thighs.

Kirkland desperately grabbed her hands, stopping their progress. "We can't." He swallowed roughly around the lie he was about to tell. "The doctor said we can't."

The naughty smile that had been curving Caressa's soft lips gradually slid away, pulling down into a frown. Kirkland pulled her down, turning so that they lay on their sides, facing each other. Kirkland kissed her forehead, her nose, her lips. "Hush, love," he murmured. "It will be all right."

"I-I need to feel you," Caressa whispered, her cheeks coloring prettily.

Kirkland felt his stomach clench at the pleading tone in her voice. He kissed her again, softly licking her lips until they opened to him, licking deeply into the warm cavern of her mouth. Caressa moaned and grasped his face, thrusting her tongue between his lips. Kirkland raised her skirt and pulled one naked leg up and over his hip. She inhaled sharply when his fingers brushed against the soft blond curls covering her damp mound.

He pressed between the lips of her sex and firmly petted the bud of her clit. Caressa cried out and Kirkland swallowed the sound as he increased the pressure of his mouth on hers. Her leg contracted, pulling their groins together. Kirkland groaned as Caressa rubbed her belly against his erection, which was trapped tightly between them. He thrust two and then three fingers inside of her, rewarded by her undulating hips grinding harder against him.

Caressa's body clenched around his fingers and he thrust harder as she came, drenching his fingers, as he climaxed between their bodies. All the while, they continued to kiss, sharing breath and, Kirkland waxed poetically to himself, sharing their souls.

Chapter Seventeen

Caressa looked at herself in the mirror. Over the past six months her body had begun to go through many changes. Her belly was distended to the point that she had to lean back as she walked for fear she might fall forward and hurt the baby. Her breasts had grown larger but were so tender, any pressure on them hurt. Her cheeks were a little rounder due to all of the extra eating. And what she was eating! Night before last she had asked Kirkland to bring her some of the lamb they had eaten for dinner between two pieces of the sweet honeyed quick-bread the cook had laid out for breakfast that morning. It had been delicious.

And her evil husband was tickled whenever she ate those unusual combinations of food. *"My father warned me. He told me my mother's favorite treat when she was having me was berries in beef gravy."*

Which, come to think of it, didn't sound so bad. Caressa made her way down stairs and headed for the back of the house to ask the cooks if they could make her such a fine delicacy. She stopped to allow two footmen carrying large potted trees to the ballroom to pass her. The party to celebrate the coming of the baby was this evening. Looking out one of the tall windows at the front door, she realized the guests were likely to begin arriving very soon as it was already growing dark. *Perhaps the cooks will be too harried.* Caressa shrugged deciding all she could do was ask.

As she passed Konnor's office, she was caught by the sound of Kirkland's voice. What she heard nearly tore out her heart.

*   *   *

Kirkland was slumped in one of the leather chairs set before his father's desk, looking back and forth between his parents. The past few months had been trying, to say the least. After that one last morning in Caressa's bed, he had kept his distance at night. He would sit with her until she fell asleep before slipping away and sleeping in his own bed on the other side of the suite. It was the only way to keep his hands to himself as he had promised himself he would.

But watching her grow heavy with the life they had created, seeing her glowing, beautiful face every day, had taxed his nerves to the limit. "You just don't understand. My entire life I was terrified of ending up in a loveless marriage – whether it be for convenience or necessity – only to get forced into one. And now, as the birth of the child gets closer and closer, I see my life spread before me with a wife who is a friend and nothing more. It's horrific."

"Kirkland, what has brought this on? When I see you and Caressa together, you seem happy. Has something happened? Is this because of your feelings for Dulcie?" His mother laid her hand atop his and squeezed gently. "Is it the prospect of her being here, of seeing her again after all this time?"

Kirkland refused to answer questions about Dulcie. Mostly because he couldn't. Whereas he wouldn't deny he had had feelings for his friend at one time, the mad passion he had felt for her as a young man was gone. She was still beautiful, he was sure, but he found the feelings of romantic love had been erased over the course of his marriage.

Now he harbored a burning love for a woman whom he had never planned to marry – who had never planned to marry him. One who had barely paid attention to him before they were wed. Before he and Caressa married, most of their discourses had been done while they would dance at parties. She had never flirted with him as she had other men and now the thought caused an ache in his chest.

"Nothing has happened. So is life. I'm in a loveless marriage, just like yours."

*   *   *

Caressa couldn't listen to any more. For the first time in weeks, the urge to be sick grabbed her stomach. Hurrying from the hall,

Caressa struggled up the stairs as quickly as she could and locked herself in her room.

* * *

"Where did you get the idea your father and I don't love each other?" Beatrice asked. Her expression was a mix of shock and dismay. Kirkland's father came over and placed his hand on her shoulder.

Kirkland frowned, watching his mother clasp his father's hand. "Well... I... You never show each other affection. Not anything like I've seen from husbands and wives who are deeply in love. Your marriage was arranged by your parents – you were both in love with other people when you married." Kirkland took a deep breath, revealing his biggest piece of evidence that they didn't need to keep up their ruse for his sake. "You never had any more children. It was only ever me."

His mother sighed, the sound one of misery. "Oh, darling. Konnor and I, we're well suited for one another."

Konnor sat on the arm of the chair Beatrice occupied. "I will admit we are not people comfortable with showing our affection publicly. My father was a general as well as a baron, son, my mother a military wife. It was a strict upbringing. Your aunt and I knew we were loved but affection wasn't much displayed in our parents' household."

"Mother was raised in a convent," Kirkland's mother said. "She was taught to be the perfect lady. Father was much older than her, and I will admit, there was not much love in their house. I would, on occasion, see unaccounted for bruises on my mother. Mother and my nanny taught me to be perfectly composed in public, knowing it would please Father."

Kirkland leaned forward and took his mother's free hand. His grandfather had died when he was young and he had never heard of his cruelty. Not even his grandmother, still alive today, spoke ill of the old man. His father wiped tears from his mother's cheeks. She smiled up at him and continued. "When I was introduced to your father, I did fancy a young lieutenant. Your father had eyes for an earl's daughter. However, we knew we had little choice but to marry each other."

His father chuckled. "We did try to thwart our parents, however. We schemed together, trying to come up with a way to get what we believed we wanted. Fortunately for me, the lieutenant was a smart man and never allowed himself to be caught alone with your mother."

"The earl's daughter was good enough to be caught being intimate with a footman and a maid." Beatrice's cheeks became bright red recounting the scandalous event. "So, with those we were enamored of unattainable, we were left with one another. Not that it mattered to me. The moment I met him, I felt something shift inside of me. The more time I spent in your father's company, the more it shifted until I fell in love with him."

"When I laid eyes on your mother for the first time after returning from Oxford, I couldn't believe what a beauty she had turned into. And she was the epitome of everything a lady should be, it seemed." Konnor laughed ruefully. "Ironically, part of my attraction to the earl's daughter had been the tales I had heard about her. But I knew, almost from the start, that I would marry your mother for more than obligation. She made me love her, and for that I will always be grateful."

His mother's and father's eyes locked, both of them smiling. When his mother looked back to him, her smile turned sad. "We wanted more children. Not because you're not perfect," she was quick to assure him. "But I lost one child before you were born and three children after. We would have loved to give you brothers and sisters, but it wasn't meant to be."

Kirkland couldn't believe what he was hearing, but the truth of their words was there before him. His parents didn't suffer a loveless marriage, but thrived in one full of love and passion. Their love was quiet but strong.

Maybe there was hope, then. Maybe Caressa could come to love him as he had come to love her.

Chapter Eighteen

Caressa pulled the cool, damp cloth from her eyes and looked into the mirror. Some of the puffiness had gone and all of the redness. There was a knock on the door and she patted her face dry before nodding to Maisy, signaling her to open the door. Kirkland stepped in and her maid left with a short curtsy to him.

Caressa looked up, looking at his reflection as he came to stand behind her. Kirkland picked up the sapphire necklace he had brought her from London. When he had given her the gift, Caressa had thought it beautiful, a sign that his feelings for her were turning. Now, as it was raised before her she saw it for what it was, a garish leash meant to appease her. She didn't want it but let him encircle her neck with it, marking her as Kirkland's. But not truly, for Kirkland didn't want her.

His hands cupped her shoulders. "Are you all right, love?"

Her heart seized at the endearment, wishing so much that it was true. Not trusting herself to speak, she nodded and allowed him to take her hand and escort her down to the ballroom. When Bowers announced them as the people of the hour, Caressa forced a smile to her face. Looking around the room, she saw Dulcie and Jack standing with Caressa's family. Dulcie gave a little wave, sadness overwhelming her features when Caressa found it impossible to return the gesture.

Caressa had neither seen or written to Dulcie since her last visit to Torningate. Caressa knew the circumstances of her marriage were not Dulcie's fault but that didn't stop the spark of pain when she looked at the woman. Kirkland's damning silence when Beatrice asked if his concern was due to Dulcie's presence just further condemned Dulcie – unfairly or not.

They wove through the crowd of well-wishers, accepting belated congratulations on their nuptials as well as for the upcoming birth of their child. When they reached Caressa and Kirkland's families, Caressa's brother's each took a turn at awkwardly hugging her. Normally they grabbed her up, lifting her off her feet as they squeezed the breath from her body. Now, with her belly protruding, they seemed at a loss.

Kirkland turned her toward Dulcie and Jackson. The taller woman had tears in her eyes but a smile on her face. "Congratulations, Caressa. I know you will be a wonderful mother." Her voice was barely above a watery whisper. "Excuse me," she murmured and walked away.

Jackson looked down at Caressa. "She's misses you, Caressa. I know what happened and I know my wife would beg your forgiveness. It would make her so happy if you would give it."

Jackson looked to Kirkland. The skin around his mouth tightened almost imperceptibly. "Congratulations, Kirk." The men shook hands and Kirkland grunted. When Jackson left to find his wife, Kirkland shook out his hand and massaged his knuckles. So Jackson did know what had happened, then. Caressa bit the inside of her cheek, forcing herself not to smile.

As the night wore on, Caressa was forced to sit and relieve her feet. Kirkland continued on through the party-goers. It wasn't long before she lost sight of her husband. She toyed with the center stone of the necklace that sat in the dip of her collarbone. Though they had been lying against her skin for hours, the stones had picked up no warmth, they were still as cold as the day Kirkland had given them to her. She wished she could tear it from her throat but she would not do something that would so publicly embarrass her husband.

Insisting on doing as much as she could without assistance, Caressa stood and headed for the buffet table, needing something to wet her parched throat. When she saw Kirkland and Dulcie talking to each other, Dulcie's hands flying in large gestures and showing her exasperation, Caressa had to force herself not to scream. The pain and anger that gripped her blinded her to everyone else in the room.

Caressa hurried from the room, away from the pair that caused her so much pain. She sought refuge in Beatrice's solar, throwing herself onto one of the chaise lounges set against the huge wall of windows. Caressa was crying so hard she didn't realize she was not alone in the room until a hand touched her shoulder.

Squeaking in surprise, Caressa looked up to find the Viscount of Godfrey standing over her. "G-good evening, Viscount." Caressa wiped at her burning cheeks. "Are you enjoying the party?"

"Mmm, it's very nice." He looked down at her. When his eyes lingered on her breasts, Caressa rose from the chaise, looking to put some distance between the viscount and herself. He followed her step for step.

"Well, I really must be getting back. Kirkland will be looking for me." She hurried to the door as fast as her new girth would allow. The viscount cut off her escape. Caressa gasped in pain as the man gripped her arms cruelly.

"He is otherwise occupied. Now, why don't you be a good little girl and get on your knees?" He twisted her arms and pulled down until her legs gave out beneath her. When the man twined his hand in her hair and yanked her head back, Caressa screamed as loud as she could.

The viscount slapped her so hard she fell to the floor. Free of him, Caressa screamed again as she scrambled away from her attacker. He advanced on her, unbuttoning the placket of his trousers. "You like being punished, don't you, lovely? I'm going to tie you to my bed and whip you until you sing out in exquisite pain."

The viscount's words were spoken seductively as though he truly believed it were an attractive prospect. Caressa found herself wedged into a corner, the viscount right in front of her. Caressa screamed again but her throat was raw and the viscount struck again, his large fist connecting with her jaw.

"Caressa!" She heard Kirkland's voice trying to break through the waves of black dragging her under.

* * *

"Get away from her!" Kirkland pulled Godfrey away from Caressa. He had gone looking for his wife after he and Dulcie had had a chance to speak. When Dulcie told him that Caressa had seen the kiss they shared that night so many months ago, Kirkland felt his heart trip. The second he had stepped out of the ballroom, a piercing cry had shot down the hall.

Kirkland had run to his mother's solar to find Godfrey standing over Caressa, his fist colliding with her chin. Kirkland threw the man to the ground and felt even more anger roll through him when he saw his cock standing out of his open trousers. Kirkland fell on him, punching him again and again, banging the viscount's head into the floor.

Arms wrapped around his shoulders and dragged him from the unconscious man. "Kirkland!" Jack shook him and turned him so they looked each other in the eye. "Stop! He's down. If you kill him, you're done for. Do you understand?"

Kirkland tried to pull away but Jackson spun him to see Caressa. Dulcie held his shaking wife in her arms. She petted Caressa's hair, murmuring gentle words, reassuring her that she was safe. "You stopped him from attacking her. But if you do not stop, now, before you kill him, you will never see her again. Never hold her again. You will never see your child. He is not worth ruining your life with Caressa."

Kirkland dropped to his knees beside them, taking Caressa from Dulcie. The fear was slow to drain from him but at least he held his Caressa in his arms. He never had to let her go.

He held his wife close, pressing kisses everywhere he could. Caressa clutched him in return. "Shh, my love, I won't let him near you ever again."

Caressa began shaking harder. Sobs wracked her body. Kirkland settled onto the floor and pulled Caressa onto his lap. "Please, love, let me know you're all right."

"Stop it," she cried. "Stop calling me love. You don't love me. You never will. I know that so just stop."

Kirkland gently cupped her face and tilted her head back so that he could look into her eyes. He felt tears sting his eyes as he took in her bruised jaw and pained eyes. He kissed the tears from her cheeks. "You're wrong, love. I do love you. I wish I could tell you I loved you from the start. That I always did. But I can tell you that I love you now. I fell in love with you somewhere along the way and I hope to God you can forgive me for being such a simpleton."

Caressa buried her fingers in his hair. "Say it again. Make me feel it."

Careful not to cause her any more pain, Kirkland pressed his lips to hers. He kissed her deeply but softly, letting his tongue feather against her lips, her tongue, the roof of her mouth. Against her lips he whispered, "I love you, Caressa. More than anything. More than I ever thought it was possible to love another person. I love you."

Caressa pulled him in for another kiss, full of the passion he had come to associate with her. "I love you, too."

Shouting erupted behind them and Caressa ducked her head, tucking herself as deeply into his lap as she could, hiding from her attacker. "Darling, I have to take care of this. I will be right back."

"No, please, just hold me." Caressa dug her fingers into his arms, holding on to him with all of her desperate strength. Much as it broke his heart to do so, he pulled her arms from around himself and urged her to let Dulcie hold her. Dulcie rocked them back and forth, singing very softly to Caressa, trying her best to sooth her.

When he rose and turned to the Viscount, he was poking Konnor in the chest. "You and that monster you call a son are in trouble deep, Perry. I will make certain the King hears of this."

"And I will make certain His Majesty hears of how you tried to rape the married daughter of a duke. Perhaps that will finally convince His Majesty to look into the servant women who have mysteriously gone missing from your estate." Kirkland closed in on Godfrey.

"Their little lives might not have meant anything to His Majesty but a viscount attacking the daughter of one of His closest friends? That will mean a great deal to the King – a much greater deal than a few bruises on such a lowly creature as you. And I promise you, if you ever come near my wife again, nothing and no one will stop me from taking your life." He looked down on Godfrey from his superior height. As Kirkland watched the man pale beneath his threat, he smiled. "Do you understand me?"

"P-p-perfectly." Godfrey ran from the room, looking back over his shoulder to make certain Kirkland wasn't following him.

Kirkland returned to where he left Caressa in Dulcie's care. He encouraged Caressa to stand. She wrapped her arms around his waist and let him take her from the room. He guided her upstairs and into his room where he carefully undressed her. He told her to get into bed. He left the room, sprinting across the suite and into her bedchamber.

Kirkland pulled clothing from her armoire and carried it to his own chamber. Caressa's eyes went enormous at the sight of him carrying an armful of ribbons and lace into his room. He dropped the dresses onto one of the chairs that banked the floor to ceiling window through which moonlight streamed.

He went back again and again until a large pile of dresses, chemises, slippers and more covered the chair and the surrounding floor. "From now on, you will sleep in here with me. I'll not spend another night alone when I am married to the woman I love and can have her in my arms."

Caressa giggled and nodded. Her arms opened and she tipped her head to one side. "Come to me, Kirkland. Please? I need you."

Chapter Nineteen

Caressa watched as Kirkland shed his clothes as quickly as he could. As he settled next to Caressa, he caught her mouth in a deep kiss. She knew that he could not make love to her as much as they both would like to. Kirkland kissed her swollen breasts, sucking very gently on her nipples. Caressa gasped and scratched his back. The feeling was almost painful but exquisite.

When she felt Kirkland's fingers slide over her sex, she cried out. He barely touched her core before her sex contracted and she cried out his name. She had been waiting so long for him to return to her and now that he had, Caressa's body sang a joyous refrain.

Kirkland pulled back, chuckling. He looked down into her eyes and Caressa blushed. "Sorry," she whispered.

"Don't be sorry. That your body craves my touch so much that I can make you cry out by barely even touching you is like a dream." He kissed her again and continued to slide his fingers over her sensitive clit, into her aching channel.

Caressa began to breathe hard. She reached down, clamping her hand around his wrist. She could feel her body beginning to tighten again. Kirkland rose above her again, looking into her eyes as her climax grew nearer and nearer. "I love you, Caressa." He whispered the words and she tipped over the edge.

"I love you!" Caressa cried out at the top of her lungs, screaming her love for the man in her arms.

Chapter Twenty

Caressa sat, exhausted, in the middle of her and Kirkland's bed. Maisy had cleaned her, wiping away the sweat five hours of pushing and straining had created. In her arms she held Eloisa Jayne Perry. Caressa smiled. Her sweet little daughter was covered in fine dark hairs, a thick mop of brown curls covering just the very top of her head. She was somewhat strange to look upon, really, but the midwife had told her the dark hair would leave her tiny body after a time. Caressa didn't care, she loved the precious bundle in her arms, no matter what she looked like. Strange or not, Eloisa was the most beautiful thing Caressa had ever seen.

Kirkland poked his head inside the room. Apparently Maisy had finally ended her sentry duty outside the bedroom door. When Caressa smiled, he entered, coming to sit beside her on the bed. He looped his arm around her shoulders and looked down at their daughter. "Such a shame," he said, shaking his head.

Caressa looked up to see him smiling. "What is?"

"Well, she's a girl, isn't she? That means we will have to keep trying." A look of pure wickedness came over his face and Caressa laughed quietly.

"I suppose we will." She sighed dramatically. "You're correct. It is a horrible shame."

Kirkland laughed and kissed her, deep and hard. "I love you. And I love her." Kirkland reached into his pocket, pulling out a beautiful necklace.

It was a cameo of two people, a man and a woman, looking at each other. Kirkland unhooked the closure and reconnected it behind her neck. She looked down at it where it lay on her breast. "What is this for?"

Kirkland kissed her on her crown and stroked a circle around the cameo. "I want to show you that I am going to spend the rest of our lives courting you as I should have. Even when we are old and gray, I hope I can make you feel as young and loved as you are."

Caressa looked up into his face, her smile so wide her cheeks hurt. Kirkland returned her smile and dipped his head, kissing her again. Caressa had never been so happy. Caressa had everything she could possibly want and she looked forward to the lifetime to come.

I am the second of four children raised in a very Catholic (clergy in the family and everything) predominantly Irish family. We are a crazy lot with ups and downs and cursing and yelling for cursing, but there is always love. I have two nephews and a niece that I adore. I was born and raised in New Jersey until my family moved to Virginia when I was fifteen. When I was twenty-four I moved to Florida but ended up missing my family and friends and moved back home to Virginia after a year and a half. I haven't travelled the world over except through the thousands of books I have read – most of which are romance novels.

I love reading romance and began writing when I was twelve. Of course, back then my writing was innocent with hand holding, hugs, and pecks on the cheek. My style has matured considerably since then. Most of my heroines share a common thread. They're not perfect by today's standards of model beauty. I don't believe a woman has to be a size zero to be beautiful. And while not all of my heroines will be on the heartier side, they all have heart. As do my heroes.

Contact info:
Website: www.sjronayne.com
email: sjronayne@sjronayne.com

Breinigsville, PA USA
16 May 2010
238043BV00002B/5/P

9 780984 461530